"There's a stranger's car out there," Jacob said.

"What? What's going on?"

His dad looked to his mom for a second then to Jacob. "Hide," he ordered. "Hide in your closet. Behind the clothes."

"Is it them?" his mama cried.

His dad nodded, his eyes so big Jacob thought they looked like the full moon he liked so much.

Jacob's heart pounded the way it did when he rode his bike up and down the street really fast over and over.

His mama pushed him toward his closet. "Hide," she repeated. "Don't come out for any reason. No matter what you hear." She hugged him. "I love you, Jacob."

"What's—" he tried to ask, but couldn't get the words out. His heart pounded; his legs felt shaky. He was scared. What was happening?

I've lived in Tennessee for nearly twenty years. It's a beautiful state. Setting a story here is always fun. I particularly love creating a small town and dropping it onto the map in one of my favorite locations. Chattanooga is a very unique city with a terrific blend of old and new. Lookout Mountain and the surrounding communities are equally unique. I've always been fascinated with the legend of Dread Hollow so I decided to create a community with that name. I've also taken certain liberties with my sheriff's department substation. I loved every minute of it and hope you will as well! Happy reading!

DISAPPEARANCE IN DREAD HOLLOW

USA TODAY Bestselling Author

DEBRA WEBB

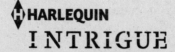

HARLEQUIN
INTRIGUE

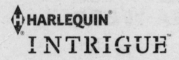

ISBN-13: 978-1-335-58271-3

Disappearance in Dread Hollow

Copyright © 2023 by Debra Webb

Recycling programs
for this product may
not exist in your area.

Harlequin Enterprises ULC
22 Adelaide St. West, 41st Floor
Toronto, Ontario M5H 4E3, Canada
www.Harlequin.com

Printed in U.S.A.

Debra Webb is the award-winning *USA TODAY* bestselling author of more than one hundred novels, including those in reader-favorite series Faces of Evil, the Colby Agency and Shades of Death. With more than four million books sold in numerous languages and countries, Debra has a love of storytelling that goes back to her childhood on a farm in Alabama. Visit Debra at debrawebb.com.

Books by Debra Webb

Harlequin Intrigue

Lookout Mountain Mysteries

Disappearance in Dread Hollow

A Winchester, Tennessee Thriller

In Self Defense
The Dark Woods
The Stranger Next Door
The Safest Lies
Witness Protection Widow
Before He Vanished
The Bone Room

Colby Agency: Sexi-ER

Finding the Edge
Sin and Bone
Body of Evidence

Faces of Evil

Dark Whispers
Still Waters

Visit the Author Profile page at Harlequin.com.

CAST OF CHARACTERS

Tara Norwood—As the deputy sheriff in Dread Hollow, life is pretty calm—until a rash of burglaries evolve into missing persons.

Deke Shepherd—Can't shake the way he feels about Tara. He wants her back. When the parents of one of his students goes missing, he and Tara are thrown together and the tension explodes.

Jacob Callaway—His parents are missing and he just wants to find them. But is he telling the whole truth?

Special Agent Jim Hanson—He's waited a very long time to solve a thirty-year-old cold case, but can he escape the personal connection?

Wilma Hambrick—The town busybody. The woman wants Dread Hollow to become an official town with a real police department and a city council. Her motive is simple: she wants to be mayor.

Tarrance Norwood—Tara's father was the sheriff of Hamilton County for thirty years, but now a disease is stealing his memories and his ability to think. Can he help Tara solve this case before it's too late?

Jeff Callaway—What did he do that put his family in danger? Is the kidnapping his way of solving his financial woes?

Chapter One

Valley Lane
Dread Hollow, Tennessee
Sunday, April 30, 7:00 p.m.

"Mama!"

"It's almost done, sweetie. Five more minutes."

Jacob stared out the window. It would be completely dark soon. They didn't get many visitors, but there was a black car parked in front of their house. He had noticed it a few minutes ago when he went to the window to see if he could see the moon. He couldn't remember if the full moon was tonight or tomorrow night, but he wanted to make sure he saw it.

"Mama!" he shouted again. "Come here!"

Jelly Bug raised her head and whined.

"It's okay, girl," Jacob said. He hadn't meant to scare the dog with his hollering.

His dad wasn't home yet. He was usually home by dark. Probably would be soon. He wouldn't miss supper. Mama had said he'd gone to fill up his truck with gas. He always did that on Sundays. Getting ready for the work week, he would say. Except he usually did it earlier in the afternoon.

His mama came to his door. "What is it, son? Supper is done, and your dad just pulled up."

Jacob peered out the window. Saw his dad's truck this time. The black car was still sitting there. The windows were too dark for him to see inside. The windows had that tinted stuff on them. Maybe whoever was inside was coming in with his dad. Could have been waiting for him to get here. Jelly Bug nudged up to Jacob's side. He patted the dog's head and turned his face up to his mom.

"There's a stranger's car out there," Jacob said, feeling like a grown-up since he'd pointed out a possible problem. His parents had taught him to be aware of strangers.

Tired, his mama sighed. She always looked tired. She worked too hard. Still, she walked over to his window. "What car?"

"That one." He pointed beyond the curtain.

"Kris!" his dad shouted from the living room.

Jacob and his mama shared a startled look at the worry in his father's voice.

His dad burst into Jacob's bedroom. He looked scared. Scared real bad. Jacob's heart beat faster like he'd started running when he was just standing still at the window.

Jelly Bug whined, and this time she shivered as if she understood something was wrong.

Jacob's mama backed away from the window. "What? What's going on?"

His dad looked to her for a second then to Jacob. "Hide," he ordered. "Hide in your closet. Behind the clothes."

"Is it them?" his mama cried.

His dad nodded, his eyes so big Jacob thought they looked like the full moon he liked so much.

Jacob's heart pounded now the way it did when he rode his bike up and down the street really fast over and over.

His mama pushed him toward his closet. "Hide," she repeated. "Don't come out for any reason. No matter what you hear." She hugged him. "I love you, Jacob."

"What's—" he tried to ask, but couldn't get the words out. His heart pounded, his legs felt shaky. He was scared. What was happening?

Jelly Bug whined some more and barked softly.

"Stay in there." His dad picked him up and set him behind the clothes in the back corner of his closet. "Don't make a sound and don't come out no matter what. Love you, son."

"What about Jelly Bug?"

"Don't worry about the dog. She'll be fine."

The door shut, but Jacob could still hear his mama making crying sounds. What was going on? Tears rolled down his cheeks. He didn't understand. Why did he have to hide?

He wanted to run after them…to call out.

But they'd told him not to...he had to stay hidden and be quiet.

He held his breath, tried to slow the racing in his chest. Tried to control the sounds trying to escape his mouth. *Be quiet! Be quiet!*

Jacob curled into himself, his knees hugged to his damp face, and rocked gently. The way his mama used to rock him when he was little. Don't make a sound. *Don't make a sound. Not one sound.*

He stilled. Heard his dad's voice. In the living room. He sounded far away, but that was because the door was closed.

Jacob stretched his neck, listened harder.

His dad was yelling now. His mama too, except her voice was quieter. She was afraid. It sounded like she was begging. Jelly Bug was barking.

Please...please don't hurt my parents.

More voices. Not so loud but deep. Men. Definitely men. Didn't sound like women.

Men from the black car. *Strangers.* People who wanted to hurt his family.

Jelly Bug was barking louder now.

Jacob closed his eyes tightly and prayed.

He prayed and prayed and prayed.

Then the house was quiet.

But he didn't move. His dad had said to stay in the closet no matter what he heard.

The sound of Jelly Bug sniffing at his bedroom door had him daring to ease out of the closet. He crawled over and sat on his knees at his bedroom door for a while, listening, afraid to open it but wanting to let Jelly Bug in. Finally, he held his breath and just did it. He opened the door without making a sound. *Whew!*

Jelly Bug wiggled around him as if trying to tell him something or just glad to see him. He didn't hear or see anything, but he wasn't taking any chances. He quietly closed the door and crawled back to the closet, closed that door too and held Jelly Bug close. She licked his face. He snuggled against her, wishing his parents would walk into his room and tell him to come out, come out, the way they did when they played the hiding game. He liked playing games with his parents. He didn't have any brothers and sisters, but he was okay with that since his parents played with him so much.

He stayed in the closet so long he fell asleep. When he woke up, his legs and arms hurt from being curled together so tight for so long.

He stretched. Groaned. Jelly Bug did the same.

For a long while, he listened but there was still no sound.

Being really careful, he reached up and opened the closet door. His room was dark now. He crawled out. Too afraid to stand up yet. If he didn't move too fast, no one would see him in the dark. Jelly Bug stayed close.

It didn't sound like anyone was here.

He wanted to call out for his mama, but he kept

his mouth closed tight. He wasn't supposed to make a sound.

At his bedroom door, he held still and listened again. The only sound was Jelly Bug's panting.

The whole house was dark. And quiet.

He held his breath as he opened the door, then eased into the hall. Jelly Bug moved with him. Maybe while he was asleep the strangers had left and his parents had gone to bed.

He stood and took a few steps forward. His legs complained as he walked after being curled up so long. He moved quietly, careful not to make a sound on the hardwood floor. He went into his parents' room, but it was too dark to see. He didn't dare turn on the light. Instead he walked to the bed and climbed into it. He moved all around the bed, but it was empty. He checked under the bed and then in their closet to see if they were hiding.

Nope.

Then he walked soundlessly to the bathroom, then the living room and finally the kitchen. No one was in the house. Just him.

Had his parents gone with the strangers?

Maybe there was a job his parents had to do. Since he'd fallen asleep, maybe they decided not to bother him.

The supper sat on the stove. He could smell the beans and ham. His stomach rumbled. He climbed into a chair at the table and waited in the darkness.

When his parents came back, they would all have supper together and go to bed.

Jacob waited. Jelly Bug waited with him.

He waited a very long time. Drifted off to sleep once and almost fell out of the chair. He shook his head. Blinked over and over. He had to stay awake so he'd know when his parents came home.

He sat in the chair so long his butt felt numb.

His stomach growled so much he was sure the neighbors would hear it.

He was starving. His mama wouldn't want him to be hungry. He hoped his parents weren't hungry.

Eventually he couldn't wait any longer. He pushed his chair over to the sink, trying to stay quiet, but it wasn't easy. He got a bowl from the drainer where his mama put the dishes when she washed them. He grabbed a spoon too. Then he pushed his chair to the stove and filled his bowl with the beans and pieces of ham floating in the soup.

Jelly Bug barked and jumped around, so he made a bowl for her too.

He sat down in the chair right there by the stove and ate.

His parents would be home soon. They would be proud of him for taking care of his supper.

When he finished, he put his and Jelly Bug's bowls in the sink and pushed his chair back to the table. He and Jelly Bug went into the living room and sat in the darkness to wait.

His mama and dad would be home any minute now. They had never left him alone.

Except that once…

Chapter Two

Deke Shepherd could no longer deny there was a serious problem with one of his students. As a teacher, it was part of his job to pay attention to the well-being of his students. Part of that included making observations about a child's general appearance and emotional state.

Case in point, last school term he noticed one of his students appeared to be having accident after accident. In October, it was a fracture of the humerus. December brought on a second-degree burn of the right hand. Then it was the mostly hidden bruises and lacerations. There came a point when Deke had to wonder if there was more than clumsiness at play.

Elementary-school students could be accident-prone or, perhaps more accurately, unaware of their limitations. Like trying out power tools or climbing ladders left unattended. Worse, playing with an un-secured handgun or rifle. Tragedy was often buried in good intentions or ill-fated distraction.

Fortunately, Deke's current concern wasn't any-thing nearly so heartbreaking—at least on the sur-face. Jacob Callaway had worn the same clothes to school three days in a row. It was obvious that he hadn't bathed either. Judging by the way he scarfed down his lunch, he likely wasn't getting breakfast at home. Sadly, there were children who were neglected all over the world. But Jacob Callaway wasn't one of them—at least not usually. The child was always clean and well-fed. His homework was always com-plete and well-done.

Until this week.

Deke had decided this morning there was some-thing going on that needed attention. Sometimes teachers had to put on a social-worker hat. It wasn't always appreciated, but it was at times necessary.

The dismissal bell rang, and the rows of third graders buzzed to life, grabbing backpacks and scrambling to escape the confines of the classroom.

When Jacob hurried to the front of his row and would have followed the throng out the door, Deke said, "Jacob, hold up a minute."

The boy froze. His wide-eyed gaze filled with uncertainty. "Am I in trouble?"

Deke felt instant regret for worrying the kid. "Course not." He produced a grin. "You never get into trouble."

It was true. Jacob was one of the most well-behaved nine-year-olds Deke had had the pleasure of teaching.

Deke propped a hip against his desk, adopting a more relaxed stance in hopes of putting the kid at ease. "Is everything okay at home?"

Jacob's eyes shuttered. "I don't know what you mean."

"Your mom and dad okay? Nobody's sick or anything like that?"

The boy's head wagged side to side in a no.

Deke considered a different avenue. "Have your mom and dad been working a lot of hours lately? Maybe getting home really late and leaving extra early?"

His shoulders went up as if he might shrug, then froze. "I...think...so."

Deke had attempted to call first the boy's mother, then father. The calls had gone straight to voice mail. He had decided a home visit was in order. Something was wrong here, and he wasn't waiting another day to determine the problem.

"Why don't I give you a ride home?" Deke reached for his briefcase. He'd already tucked away the papers he needed to grade and prepared for leaving at the same time as his students.

Jacob's shoulders drooped. "'Kay."

The boy didn't ride a bus. He either walked or one of his parents picked him up. Since he didn't mention the possibility that one or the other would be picking him up, Deke assumed that wasn't going to happen.

He flipped off the classroom light as they exited. The school was a kindergarten through twelfth grade institution. It was small and Deke liked it that way. He'd put in his time at one of the big schools in Chattanooga. The move to this small community had been the best decision of his career. He paused at his truck and opened the door for his passenger. Or maybe it had been more about his personal life than his career. He'd been ready for peace and quiet. Whatever. Three years later, he was still happy with his decision.

Jacob looked up at him. "You sure I'm not in trouble, Mr. D?"

"You have my word, Jacob. You are not in trouble with me," he promised.

The boy climbed into the old Ford. The truck had belonged to Deke's father. It was the one useful thing the old man had left him. When Deke had made the decision to leave the city, he'd left his sports car and his downtown condo to new owners. He was perfectly happy in the old farmhouse he was still renovating and the truck his father had driven for thirty years. Truth was the truck looked better than the farmhouse. His father had been like that, kept everything organized and in tip-top shape. He just hadn't been very good at relationships.

Not that Deke could claim he was much better. At thirty-five, he was a work-in-progress, but he was getting there.

Deke glanced at his passenger as he waited his

turn to exit the school parking lot. "You ready for the social studies test tomorrow?"

Jacob glanced at him. "Yes, sir."

"Good." Deke smiled. He'd expected the answer. Jacob was a good student. Until yesterday he'd never failed to turn in his homework. Every kid deserved a pass now and then.

The crossing guard waved him forward, and Deke allowed the truck to roll out onto the street. Dread Hollow was a small community carved out of Lookout Mountain, only miles above the fray in Chattanooga. The area was surrounded by attractions, like the haunted house named after Dread Hollow. But the Hollow remained a small, isolated village deep in the woods, away from the high-end real estate only a few miles away.

Deke slowed for the turn from Main Street onto Hillside Drive. There was a post office, a diner, a small market and a walk-in health clinic. Plus, the school of course. The Hollow wasn't big enough for its own police department, but there was a substation of the sheriff's department. The sheriff's deputy in charge was a regular at career day and anti-drug programs at the school.

He excised the thought of the deputy, his most recent fail at relationships.

Granted that fumble had been his first since moving to the Hollow. He'd avoided relationships for two full years, and then he'd fallen face first. It had ended quickly enough. Too quickly for him. He still had no idea where he'd gone wrong. For once, he'd thought the relationship was going well.

Deke navigated from Hillside Drive to Valley Lane. Jacob lived in the last house on the left. The vehicle he'd seen Jacob's mother driving when she dropped him off at school sat in the driveway. Like the houses on this short lane, the car had seen better days. Deke parked behind it.

Jacob seemed to sink deeper into the seat.

"Looks like your mom is home," Deke commented as he shut off the engine and reached for the door handle.

Jacob didn't respond, just popped his seat belt, opened the door and slid out.

Deke followed him up the drive, past the parked car. He glanced inside. No overnight bag suggesting his mom had been on a trip. No trash indicating extended travel. Nothing out of place.

The steps creaked as they climbed to the narrow porch. Jacob led the way, reaching beneath his shirt for a necklace that held a key. He unlocked the door, glanced back at Deke and then went inside.

The dread on the child's face was unmistakable. Deke's gut tightened. Braced for trouble.

"Mama!" Jacob called out.

A small tan dog, maybe a cross between a dachshund and a cocker spaniel jumped around the boy and yipped.

Deke lingered near the door. Since he hadn't

knocked, he decided it was best that he didn't venture inside until he had an adult's permission.

Jacob disappeared into another room, calling for his mother again, then his dad.

The house was dead silent. No smells of recently cooked food though there was an underlying stench suggesting the trash was overdue to be removed. The house was stuffy as if the air conditioning was off. Windows in the living room were closed.

Jacob reappeared. "I guess they're not home yet."

"Why don't we call your mother's workplace and see if she's still there?" Deke suggested.

"She doesn't like for me to call the diner unless it's an emergency." He scrunched up his face. "She might get into trouble."

He stared up at Deke as if the idea of calling his mother's workplace was scarier than the possibility of being home alone—which Deke suspected he may have been all week.

"I'm afraid you can't stay home alone," Deke countered. Tennessee law suggested the age of ten for a child being left home alone. A parent might be able to decide otherwise, but as the kid's teacher, Deke didn't have that leeway.

The kid tossed his backpack on the sofa and shrugged. "I always stay home alone when my parents have to work late. I can take care of myself."

"Let's talk a minute," Deke suggested. He walked to the sofa and sat down.

Jacob shuffled over to a chair and sat down, shoulders slumped once more.

"I noticed you've been wearing that same T-shirt and jeans all week."

Jacob stared down at his clothes but said nothing.

"You didn't have your homework yesterday or today," Deke went on. "That's a little out of character, Jacob. You always have your homework."

"My mom has been working a lot of hours and…" He glanced around as if trying to decide where to go next with his explanation. "My dad is out of town."

This was certainly possible. These days folks did whatever necessary to maintain a decent income.

"Did you see your mother before school this morning?"

Jacob hesitated but then shook his head. "She was already gone."

But why wasn't she home now? Her car was in the driveway. Deke let that go for a moment. "Did you see her last night before you went to bed?"

Again he shook his head. "I was asleep already."

"Then how do you know she was home at all?"

"Course she was home."

"Does she drive to work?" Deke asked.

Jacob nodded. "Sure."

"Her car is in the driveway," Deke pointed out.

The kid chewed at his lip a second or two. "I think she went with my dad today."

"I thought he was out of town." Deke hated making the boy uncomfortable.

Jacob's hands knotted together. "He must have come home today." He scooted to the edge of his seat. "I have to feed Jelly Bug and take her out."

Deke might be reaching here, but he had to do something. He couldn't simply accept the kid's explanations and let it go. "Do you mind if we go to the kitchen? I really need a drink of water."

Jacob twisted his hands tighter, then nodded. "Sure."

He got up and shuffled toward the next room. Deke pushed to his feet and followed. The living room appeared ordinary. Neat. Nothing fancy. The few houses on this street were old, most visibly in need of repairs. The furniture was well worn but clean. Jacob's parents had made the best of what they had.

The kitchen on the other hand was anything but tidy. A jar of peanut butter sat open on the counter. A partial loaf of bread stood along with a half-eaten bag of chips. Crumbs and used utensils were scattered about. There were dirty dishes—cups, glasses, cereal bowls—in the sink.

A pot of beans sat on the stove. Judging by the smell, it had been there a couple of days anyway. Deke's concern moved up several notches.

"You've been making your own dinner?" Deke watched the boy's face. Spotted the deer caught in the headlights look.

Jacob nodded.

"Okay, you need to be completely honest with me here. Where's your mom, Jacob?"

His lower lip trembled. "I don't know."

Deke's gut tightened. "What about your dad?"

The kid's head swung side to side. "I don't know."

Deke crouched down to his eye level. "When did you last see either one of them?"

"Sunday." He shrugged. "Close to dark. The moon was almost out."

"They didn't come home Sunday night?"

"No."

"Did they leave in your dad's truck?"

Another sad shake of his head. "Two men came to the house."

Tension filtered through Deke. "Did you know the men?"

"Mama made me hide in the closet when she saw them outside. I never saw them."

"So, whoever these men were," Deke began, "your mother was afraid of them or something like that?"

He nodded. "She was scared. She told me to stay hidden no matter what I heard, and I did."

Deke braced for more bad news. "What did you hear, Jacob?"

"Shouting." He glanced at the floor. "Bad words."

"You didn't recognize the voices?"

"No. Just my parents begging for them to leave."

"Did they say anything that might tell us why they had come to see your folks?"

"There was a lot of yelling, but I didn't understand

what they were saying. I just know they all left. I waited up…until I fell asleep on the couch. But they never came home."

Deke considered how to phrase his next question. He didn't want to make the boy feel any worse than he already did.

"Jacob, why didn't you tell me about this when you came to school on Monday?"

He stared at the floor. "I didn't tell anyone."

"Why didn't you tell anyone?"

"This happened once before." He met Deke's gaze. "Before we moved here. Not the bad men in the black car like the other night. Just the not coming home part. My mama and dad came home really late one night because they had to work. The boss said if they left they'd get fired. I didn't know. I was little, like seven, I think. I just knew they weren't home, and I got worried and went out in the yard looking for them. A neighbor saw me and called the police. When my parents came home it didn't matter, the police wouldn't let me stay with them. It was a whole month before I got to go back home." He stared at his knotted fingers. "I don't want that to happen again. They'll be back. I know they will. It's probably work. Please don't tell, Mr. D."

Deke patted him on the shoulder. "Don't worry. We'll figure this out."

"Just don't call the police," Jacob urged. "Please don't call the police."

As badly as he didn't want to cause the child any further distress, there was no help for it.

"Look," Deke offered, "I have a friend who works at the sheriff's department. We can call her, and she'll help us find your parents. Does that sound like a good plan to you?"

Jacob's gaze narrowed. "Are you sure she's a friend?"

That could possibly be debatable, but Deke was confident she wouldn't let Jacob down. "She's a good friend. She'll do all she can to help you."

"Okay." Tears welled in his eyes. "I'm really getting worried. They've never left like this before."

"Let's take Jelly Bug out and get her fed, and I'll call my friend."

This was one time when Deke wished his instincts had been wrong.

This—whatever this was—was a serious problem.

Chapter Three

"I'm telling you, Deputy Norwood, it's the right thing to do."

Tara Norwood somehow managed to keep a smile in place as she listened to Wilma Hambrick go on and on about the possibility of starting the process of forming a police department in Dread Hollow. For now, the small community was served by a substation of the Hamilton County Sheriff's Department. Until a couple of weeks ago, the arrangement had worked amazingly well.

Wilma Hambrick had other ideas. She had worked long and hard to achieve incorporation for Dread Hollow—a small community which barely met the minimum population of 1500 people required. According to Tara's dad, the woman had started the process just so she could be elected mayor. Having achieved that goal last year, her newest endeavor was to go after a police department. Just another step in the process of giving herself more power, Tara's dad insisted.

Tara didn't see the point. A fully formed city government only cost the locals more in taxes. Hiring a police chief and a couple of deputies would serve the community no better than what they had now. Tara was the sheriff's deputy in charge of the substation. Collin Porch was the only other deputy assigned full time to the substation. He lived in nearby East Ridge. Since Tara lived in Dread Hollow, she was on call 24/7. Thankfully, there wasn't enough crime or trouble of any sort in Dread Hollow to authorize additional personnel, much less an entire department. Tara couldn't remember the last time she'd had to arrest anyone. She spent more of her time finding the occasional escapee from the local assisted-living facility than she did chasing criminals.

Until, she acknowledged silently, two weeks ago when a sudden rash of burglaries started. Most of the stolen goods were basically small time. Televisions. Cell phones and other easily sold goods. No one had been caught, and Tara would have been ready to consider the work that of a group of teenagers playing dare games—except for the handful of witnesses who claimed to have seen two men dressed all in black, including ski masks. Still could be teenagers, but so far no one had ratted them out. Chances were, someone would talk eventually.

"Ms. Hambrick," she said patiently, "it's my firm

belief that decisions like this need to be made by the folks who live in Dread Hollow."

"People are talking about these burglaries and your inability to catch the perpetrators," Hambrick warned.

This was true to a degree, but it wasn't as bad as it sounded. A few people had complained.

"You live in Dread Hollow," the woman insisted. "You and your family have been here for five generations. The people listen to Norwoods. If your daddy would talk to the folks and tell them how good this would be, we could make it happen." She smiled broadly, her faded lipstick highlighting only parts of her lips. "And you would be our first chief of police."

And there it was—the real reason Wilma Hambrick was hounding Tara. Her dad's influence. No matter that he was not in the best of health, what he thought still carried weight in this community.

Tara reached deep down for more patience. "Ms. Hambrick, you know my dad doesn't get out much these days."

The fact that he had been diagnosed with second-stage Alzheimer's apparently hadn't given the woman pause. Although he had a lot of good days, there were those that were not so good, and even on his better days there were moments. The steady progression of the disease prevented him from taking care of himself without some degree of assistance.

Frustration and hurt curdled inside Tara. She'd wanted her father to live with her so she could take care of him, but he'd refused. He would not be a burden. Before she had even known the full extent of his condition, he'd made arrangements at Forrest Hills and checked himself in. Tara had been stunned and hurt, more so than she would ever tell her dad. Despite the shock of his decision, she had understood that he meant well.

Forrest Hills was just a few miles up Dread Hollow Road from the home where he and his father and his grandfather as well as his great-grandfather before that had grown up. Theirs was the first farm in the community. Forrest Hills was also the facility that occasionally had a runaway. The rare escape notwithstanding, the place was very nice. It just wasn't where Tara wanted her father.

Hambrick shook her head, her expression arranged into one of sadness. "I so hated to hear about his illness. Your daddy is a fine man. He was the best sheriff Hamilton County ever had, you know. Sheriff Decker is a good man, but he'll never be the kind of lawman your daddy was."

Tara smiled, a real one this time. "Yes, ma'am, I know."

Hambrick leaned forward in her chair. Far enough that her top-heaviness might surely topple her over at any second. "You could speak for your father. When folks see you, they think of him."

"I'll consider your request," Tara said, primarily to get her gone. She stood. "I appreciate you stopping by."

How poor Mr. Hambrick, God rest his soul, had lived with this woman for the better part of his life was beyond comprehension. Her father's words, not Tara's. Any time the Hambricks ever came up in conversation, her dad made that statement. He would say, "It's no wonder he failed to take his heart medication. It was as good a way to go as any." There were rumors that Ms. Hambrick had withheld his medication after his stroke. As annoying as the woman could be, the truth was her husband had been a controlling miser. Even as a kid, Tara had recognized he was mean. Maybe he was the reason the woman pushed her weight around. She had a lot of years of not getting what she wanted to make up for, Tara supposed.

Hambrick hoisted herself out of her chair. "You know my arthritis has been giving me a fit. All those April showers that have lingered into May. With Fred gone, I just don't know how I would protect myself if those thieves stormed into my house."

"I understand, ma'am. Keep your doors locked and the outside lights on. They seem to prefer the easier pickings."

The MO of the burglars hadn't changed so far. If Tara was lucky, the situation wouldn't escalate before the two were identified and found.

Tara followed the lady to the door and saw her out. She watched until Hambrick had driven away.

There was something else her dad would say about Wilma Hambrick. The woman could talk your ear off.

While her work in Dread Hollow was nothing like the four years Tara had served in Nashville's Metro Police Department, she didn't regret the move one little bit. Her decision to leave Nashville and to take a job with Hamilton County had come after her mother's death five years ago. Though he would never have said as much, her father had needed her. He'd retired early just so he could take care of his beloved wife through her extended illness. After her death, he'd been a little lost.

Tara had helped him through that tough time. Then she'd met someone and suddenly there was a wedding to be planned. As if the stars had abruptly all aligned, the department had decided to open a substation in Dread Hollow and offered Tara the job. No matter that she'd felt confident the work would prove a bit on the boring side, she had hoped to be starting a family right away. Dread Hollow was the perfect place for raising children. Then her father would be too busy with grandkids to be so sad all the time.

But life didn't always work out as planned.

Barely two years later, the marriage had ended. The family never happened, and her father's health had gone into decline.

The cell on her hip vibrated and Tara pushed away the unpleasant memories. If she were lucky another of Sam Brown's llamas hadn't gotten out. A couple weeks ago two of the feisty creatures had decided they liked walking Main Street. Granted the Hollow didn't have a lot of traffic, but folks got a little upset when the animals traipsed through well-manicured lawns leaving unsightly droppings and foraging on all manner of shrubs and flowering plants. Rounding up the llamas had been no picnic either.

Better escaped llamas than another burglary, she supposed.

"Deputy Norwood," she said in greeting.

The silence on the other end of the line set her senses on alert. There was the occasional call for help after a fall or someone with chest pains. Tara was closer than the fire station, so she typically received the call first.

"Hello," she prompted.

"Tara, it's Deke."

She blinked. Startled. They both lived in Dread Hollow, so not bumping into each other was impossible—hard as she tried to ensure they didn't. They even spoke occasionally in the market or on the street if they happened to cross paths. But they didn't call each other. Ever.

Before she could ask why he had called, he went on. "I'm at the home of one of my students, Jacob Callaway. He lives over on Valley Lane."

"I'm familiar with the Callaways." Tara didn't know them well, but she made it a point to be aware of folks who moved into her jurisdiction. The couple appeared to be about her and Deke's age, midthirties. The father worked at the poultry hatchery in

Hixon. The mother worked at the diner on Main. One child, Jacob.

"According to Jacob, his parents have been missing since Sunday."

"Missing?" A frown tugged at Tara's brow. It wasn't unheard of for parents to just take off and leave a child. Sadly, it happened far too often. But not here. And though Tara was only acquainted with the mother, she'd overheard the woman showing off pictures of her son and bragging about his accomplishments at school any time Tara was in the diner. The Callaway woman didn't seem like the type.

"Missing," Deke confirmed. "I noticed Jacob had been wearing the same clothes three days in a row. He insisted everything was okay at home, but when I brought him home today, it was obvious he's been making his own supper. He finally admitted they haven't been home since Sunday." He exhaled a big breath. "Look, he didn't want me to call. Apparently, something similar has happened before, and he's afraid of being separated from his parents again. I promised him that wouldn't happen this time. I told him you would make sure."

She wanted to be angry that he would make such a promise, but she knew Deke. He loved his students. He would make exactly that kind of promise if that was what it took to keep a student safe and happy.

"I'll be right there."

"Thanks, Tara. I appreciate it."

"Yeah." She ended the call and headed for her

vehicle. Since there was only one cruiser, she used her Wagoneer.

Collin Porch, the other deputy assigned to Dread Hollow, was out on patrol, so she gave him a quick call to bring him up to speed. The anticipation that instantly filled his voice was a reminder of just how calm life in Dread Hollow generally proved to be. She promised to keep him informed and headed for Valley Lane.

Main Street was home to the post office and the market as well as a handful of small locally owned and operated specialty shops. Martha Jo's Boutique, a children's and ladies' handmade goods shop. Cherry's Candle and Baked Goods. The small Feed and Seed Store, the Dreadfully Good Coffee Shop and Delilah's Diner.

In the fall, the town was full of tourists cruising through on the way to the famous Dread Hollow haunted house. It wasn't actually in their little town, but it was only a couple miles away.

There wasn't an operating gas station along Main Street, but there was a vintage one that was home to a family-owned-and-operated auto repair shop called Franklin's Fix-It. Tara had her 1987 Wagoneer serviced there, mostly because she'd graduated high school with Henry Franklin. Henry had been her best friend. Probably always would be. He knew more of her secrets than anyone—including her ex-husband. She and Henry had been quite the pranksters back in high school.

Most of the residents of the Hollow lived well off
Main. There were a couple of renovated condos over
some of the shops. At the edge of the newly incorpo-
rated town limits, an old elastic manufacturing mill
had been turned into four apartments.

Once she was on Valley Lane, Tara spotted Deke's
truck at the last house on the left and pulled to the
side of the street. There were no curbs or sidewalks.
Just a half dozen one-story ranch-style houses that
had seen better days. The houses were spaced farther apart than in most subdivisions since construc-
tion fizzled out before it was completed.

Deke and Jacob sat on the steps leading up to the
narrow porch. Tara climbed out of the Wagoneer and
put on her best smile. She wore the same navy uniform as the other Hamilton County deputies with the
matching baseball cap style headgear. Black leather
shoes and the garden-variety utility belt that held
the tools of her trade, including a baton and a service weapon.

Deke stood as she approached. Jacob did the
same. If the fear on his face was any gauge of the
terror he felt, she just wanted to hug the poor kid.
His dark eyes were wide. Dark hair was mussed and
in need of a good shampooing. Clothes were obviously in need of a wash.

The image just didn't fit with what she knew of
his mother.

But he had a father too, and Tara knew very little about him.

Worry pounded in her veins. She'd been in charge

of public safety in this little corner of the world for five years now. So far there had been no murders or grave assaults of any kind. She hoped that blessed record wasn't about to change.

"Hey, Jacob." She crouched down to a squat to give him the height advantage and then extended her hand. "You remember me from the Don't Do Drugs class last fall?"

He nodded. Shook her hand. "You brought that dog to class."

She smiled. "I did. His name is Snoopy. He's still helping my colleagues find the bad stuff."

His hand fell away. "Mr. D said you'd help me find my parents."

Tara glanced up at the teacher hovering next to the boy, suppressed the instant reaction to seeing him then returned her full attention to the kid. "I'll do everything I can. You have my word."

Jacob appeared to relax just a little. "Good. Because I know they wouldn't leave me like this unless something was wrong."

"I think you're right," Tara agreed. "I know your mom from the diner, and she's always bragging on you. Why don't we go inside and you can tell me what happened?"

"'Kay."

Jacob turned and headed into the house. Tara pushed to her feet. "Any signs of struggle in there?"

Deke shook his head. "None that I saw."

"Let's have another look."

Tara started past him and he touched her arm. She stilled. Rode out the flash of heat that seared through her even at such an innocent connection.

"Thank you for reassuring him. He's really scared."

She moved on without responding. Their shared history had no place in whatever this was.

Inside the house, Tara was greeted by a frisky dog. Once she'd given the animal some love, she glanced around. From what she could see, the place was sparsely furnished and neat. Framed photos of Jacob and his parents hung on the walls. Not studio photographs in high-end designer frames; just the kind snapped with a cell phone, printed at a chain pharmacy and displayed in faux-wood frames bought at a big-box store. Didn't matter. The moments captured told the story. Jacob was a well-loved child by both parents. The father's broad smile and big hugs would be difficult to fake.

But sometimes darkness lurked deep beneath the surface.

She shook off the idea. Too early to form an opinion.

Jacob told her about the two men who showed up at their house on Sunday. He hadn't seen their faces, just heard two distinct voices. The car they had driven was black. Before he'd seen anything more than the car in the driveway, his mom had insisted he hide until the men were gone. Except then his parents were gone too. Not a lot to go on. Two facts were clear: the parents had known the men, and they had been afraid.

Since Jacob hadn't seen the men, she wasn't ready to take the leap that the two could be the pair in black who had been breaking into houses around the Hollow. Small-time criminals often escalated to larger crimes. Part of her hoped that was not the case, but then again, if it wasn't the burglars, then who? She and Collin had concluded the burglars were locals. These perps could be anyone from anywhere…capable of anything.

"How about a tour?" Tara said to Jacob. "I like to begin with a good look around."

Jacob glanced side to side. "This is the living room." He pointed to the television hanging on the wall. "We got that for Christmas."

"Nice gift," Tara commented. It was a low-end model. Not overly expensive. She was looking for clues that the couple was living above their means. A kidnapping event was most often related to money. Either the perps wanted money or were owed money.

Jacob motioned her through a wide, cased opening. "This is the kitchen."

The dog rubbed against him. "Not now, Jelly Bug."

Tara smiled at the dog's name. "She sure does like you."

"She was a present from my mom last year. She said Jelly Bug would keep me company when she was in the hospital."

Tara glanced at Deke. "She's all better now," he told her and gave her a look that said he would explain later.

The kitchen and dining room were one room, slightly larger than the living room. The cabinets formed a peninsula that divided the two spaces. Appliances looked old but clean. Dishes in the sink and sandwich makings were scattered on the peninsula counter. A pot of days-old beans stood on the stove.

Tara checked the fridge. Mostly empty. She frowned. "When does your mom do her shopping?"

"On Mondays. That's when she gets paid."

Only this Monday she hadn't been around to shop and replenish their staples.

Tara turned to Jacob. "So where do you sleep?" She hitched her head toward the stove. "In the oven?"

"No." He laughed. "I have a bedroom."

"Let's see it then."

Jacob led the way back into the living room and into a narrow hall. Deke brought up the rear, keeping his distance. Tara was glad. She couldn't think clearly when he was too close. Confessing as much, even only to herself, was unnerving. Even her ex-husband hadn't been able to shake her up that way.

"This is my room," Jacob announced as they entered the first room on the right.

A Spider-Man comforter half-on and half-off the twin bed confirmed as much. There were somewhat crude drawings of Spider-Man on the wall. As rudimentary as the drawings were, they had definite potential.

"Did you do these?" Tara gestured to the drawings.

He nodded eagerly. "My dad says if I keep practicing, I can draw cartoons when I grow up. I won't have to work so hard like he does."

Another indication of a loving father. He wanted better for his child. "Well, I think your dad is right. These are pretty good."

A wide grin had the boy's eyes sparkling.

She made a show of checking the closet, the dresser drawers and under the bed. Jelly Bug had a bed next to Jacob's. "I don't see anything unusual here," she said. "Where do your parents sleep?"

His smile faded a bit. "This way."

She followed him out of the room. Deke had waited in the hall. She avoided eye contact. He was watching her. She didn't have to look to see that. She could feel his eyes on her. How had a mere six-month relationship so thoroughly and deeply connected her to this man?

The family bathroom was the last door on the right, and then there was the only other bedroom on the left. The bed was made. The drawers in the night tables and dresser were neatly organized. Nothing unexpected in any of them. Tara spotted no surprises at all on her sweep. The closet was the same. The parent's wardrobes were meager. Clearly they spent the bulk of whatever they had for clothing on their son. She checked under the bed. Spotted a box, maybe a shoebox, but decided not to inspect it just now. When Jacob was otherwise occupied, she'd have a look. She didn't really expect to find anything, but if his parents were hiding something perhaps intimate under the bed, she'd rather not discover it in his presence.

She stood and set her hands on her hips. "The room's clear. Why don't we go back to the living room, and you can answer a few questions for me? I'll call my partner and have him come help us look. Does that sound okay?"

Jacob nodded and headed back to the living room. When he was out of sight, she motioned for Deke to join her. When he was close—close enough for her to smell the aftershave he always wore—she explained her first impressions.

"The fact that there's no sign of a struggle and no blood gives me some hope that this might not be as bad as it looks."

The relief that flooded his face was profound. "I hope for Jacob's sake you're right."

"There's a lot we don't know yet, but I intend to keep a hopeful attitude until I have reason not to." That had been her dad's motto, and she'd adopted it when she followed his footsteps into law enforcement. "I'll let you know when I'm worried."

"I appreciate that."

"The mother was ill?"

Deke nodded. "Last year. Breast cancer."

Tara winced. "Bad stuff." She took a breath. "Can you keep Jacob distracted for a minute while I call Collin?"

"Sure."

Deke hesitated as if there was more he wanted to say, then he walked out. When she heard him talking to Jacob, she made the call. Collin would be here in ten minutes. Meanwhile, before she returned to the living room she got on her knees next to the bed and had another look beneath it.

First she pulled a pair of gloves from the pocket on her utility belt and tugged them on, then dragged the box from under the bed. She had been right—a shoebox. The memory of picking through old photos in a shoebox when she was a kid visiting her grandmother made her smile. She removed the lid and peered at the contents. Her jaw dropped, and she sat back on her heels.

Now she was worried.

Chapter Four

Tara appreciated Deke keeping Jacob occupied while she brought Deputy Collin Porch up to speed.

"Fifty thousand dollars?" Collin's eyebrows reared up. "I don't think Krissy makes tips like that at the diner."

Krissy Callaway was Jacob's mother.

"And we both know Jeff doesn't make that much at the hatchery." Some small amount over minimum wage she suspected.

"Could have been a gift from a rich uncle," Collin joked, but his face showed no amusement. He shook his head. "Whatever it is, it probably ain't legal. You think this," he nodded to the shoebox sitting on the bed, "is why they're MIA?"

That was the million-dollar—or fifty-thousand-dollar, it seemed—question.

"My first thought would be yes." She considered the neatly banded bundles of cash. Fifty bundles of hundred-dollar bills totaling one thousand per bundle. "If that's the case, why is the money still here? It's not like it was well hidden."

Collin exhaled a big breath. "I'll put out an APB on the father's truck."

Tara nodded. "Call the hatchery and see if Jeff showed up for work this week. I'm guessing not since he didn't come home after. I'll check with Delilah at the diner. See if she's heard from Krissy. Then we can start talking to the neighbors. Maybe we'll get lucky and someone saw something on Sunday."

"If we're really lucky," Collin offered, "one of them has a video doorbell or security camera that might have picked up a license plate."

They'd likely never get that lucky, but it didn't hurt to wish.

"You think this has anything to do with the burglaries?"

"At this point, I'd say no. This is way bigger than a stolen television or a nabbed cell phone."

"I guess it's just our turn for the crazies to come out," Collin suggested. "We did have a full moon on Sunday night."

"Maybe so. I'm calling headquarters and requesting a CSI team." Tara rubbed at the lines of frustration on her forehead. "Maybe we'll get lucky and find some prints that will give us some clue as to who the two men were."

Plus, the cash needed to be entered into evidence. She'd leave that to CSI as well. The sooner the place was gone over and the money was out of here, the better.

When Collin headed outside, she hesitated. At this point there was no denying that Jacob had been abandoned, whatever the circumstances. She had no choice but to make a call to Children's Services and get someone over here to take custody of Jacob. If he'd been through this before, he would know the routine. That said, being aware of the steps wasn't necessarily going to prevent him from being scared.

Her first call was to summon the CSI folks. Children's Services was next.

With the necessary balls rolling, Tara caught up with Deke and Jacob on the back porch. After finding the money, she had decided it might be better not to contaminate what was clearly a crime scene any further. Deke had grabbed a bag of chips and a bottle of water for Jacob and taken him out back. The two were seated at a ramshackle picnic table. Jelly Bug danced around the table as if keeping them entertained or hoping for a dropped chip.

Jacob looked up at her expectantly. "Did you find any clues?"

Not the sort she'd hoped for.

"Nothing that gives us any answers," she evaded. She settled on the bench on Jacob's side of the table. "Look, you know that as a deputy I have to play by certain rules when I'm investigating a case."

The boy stared at her without flinching, but the

resignation in his eyes told her he understood what was coming.

"Tara."

She shot a look at Deke. He, of all people, realized she had no choice. And he sure as hell had no right to call her by her first name at a time like this.

"Until we figure out where your parents are and bring them back home," she said to Jacob, ignoring the man now glaring at her, "you need a safe place to stay."

His small face fell from vaguely hopeful to defeat. "I'm big enough to take care of myself. I know how to make my sandwiches and…and tuck myself in at night."

Tara smiled but it hurt to do it. "You are really smart and very reliable. Mr. D tells me you're a great student, but there are rules. You have rules in school, right? So you understand that when we have rules, we have to follow them."

He nodded, a jerky motion.

"Ms. Carter from Children's Services is coming to pick you up. She'll take you to a home where you'll be safe until your parents are back." The tears that welled in his eyes ripped at Tara's gut. "The really good news is I think you know the home you'll be staying at. Ms. Wright, the nurse at your school, wants you to stay with her family until we sort this out."

He blinked back the tears. "I like Ms. Wright. Her son is in kindergarten. I know him too." The crestfallen expression returned. "But what about Jelly Bug?"

Tara nodded. "Ms. Wright said Jelly Bug can come too. Why don't we pack a bag for you to take on your adventure at Ms. Wright's house?"

"Okay!" Jacob scooted off the bench. "Come on, Jelly Bug, we gotta pack." He and his dog hustled into the house.

Tara prepared to follow him, but Deke waylaid her, his hand on her arm again. Tara rode out the reaction she couldn't seem to quell even after all this time.

"Thanks for making this as easy as it can be."

The sincerity in his eyes tugged at her. How many times had she seen those blue eyes in her dreams? No matter how hard she'd evicted thoughts of him, they just kept coming back anyway. Six damned months was a long time for a pointless yet insistent need to hang on.

"Just doing my job." She turned back to the door, but he held on tighter.

"I'm the last person you want to talk to, I get that." He dropped his hand as if suddenly realizing he shouldn't be touching her. "But I don't see why we can't be friends. Particularly at a time like this."

She shook her head, shifted her gaze away from his. "I don't know what you mean. Of course, we're friends."

Before he could argue with her statement, she hurried after Jacob.

After pajamas and a week's worth of clothes were selected, along with kibble for Jelly Bug, they went outside to meet Ms. Carter. She was young with two kids of her own, and she seemed to really connect with her clients. By the time she loaded Jacob and his dog into her SUV, he was smiling and appeared okay with the situation.

Kids were amazing.

Deep inside, where Tara never allowed anyone else to see, pain twisted. She set her senses to ignore and focused on work. Work never let her down.

Thankfully, the CSI team arrived, preventing too much time alone with Deke.

Being alone with Deke was not safe.

Once she'd filled in the two-person team, she walked to the street where Deke leaned against his truck.

"Thanks for calling me," she said. "We'll take it from here."

He gave a single resolute nod. "That's my cue to go, I guess."

She gestured to the CSI van. "They'll be pulling out the crime-scene tape any time now. Even I won't be allowed back inside until they're finished." The last part might be an overstatement, but she needed him gone. "There's really no reason for you to stay at this point."

He straightened away from the truck. "Well, it was good to see you—the circumstances notwithstanding." He shook his head, laughed softly. "It's funny.

As small as the Hollow is, you'd think we'd run into each other more often."

"You're busy," Tara offered. "I'm busy. Time gets away." Not to mention she made it a point to avoid him as much as possible.

"Guess so." He wasn't convinced. She was lying and he knew it.

Guilt pinged her. "If you would, keep a close eye on him at school and let me know if you notice any uncharacteristic behavior."

"You know I will."

She did. "Thanks."

He opened the driver's door but hesitated before getting in so that he could hold her gaze a beat longer. "Maybe one of these days you'll spell it out for me."

She frowned. "Spell what out?" The words were out of her mouth before her brain assimilated what he meant.

"What happened to us." He shrugged. "I thought we were really good together."

For three endless seconds, she couldn't speak. What the hell? Tara Norwood was a cop. She'd made it through the training. She'd dealt with some sick criminals before transferring to the Hollow. As a twelve-year-old, she'd watched her mother bleed to death while trapped by her seat belt in a vehicle hanging upside down on the edge of a cliff. Three and a half years ago, she'd gone through another kind of hell when her marriage fell apart. Now she was holding up under her father's ailing health, understanding that when he was gone she would be alone.

She was damned strong.

Yet this man…a man she'd walked away from six months and fifteen days ago…had the power to make her want to fall into his arms and cry like a baby.

Damn him.

She braced herself. Kicked aside all those weak emotions. "What did you expect? That we'd move in together? A marriage proposal?" She laughed, couldn't help herself. "That we'd live happily ever after." She shook her head. "I thought I made myself clear. I've been down that road. I didn't like the trip, and I don't intend to ever take it again. Is that clear enough?"

She didn't hang around for his response. Mostly because she couldn't bear the hurt in his eyes.

Hurt she had caused.

Main Street, 7:30 p.m.

THE DINER WAS packed when Tara arrived. She'd checked with Carter, and Jacob and Jelly Bug were safely ensconced at Brenda Wright's house. Then Tara had come to the diner to talk to Jacob's mom's employer. Every table and booth was filled. No problem. She took the only vacant stool at the counter and waited for Delilah to cruise past.

Collin had spoken to the manager and the shift leader at the hatchery. Jeff Callaway had given no indication there was trouble in his life. He'd come to work on Friday, on time like always, and they hadn't seen him since. His cell, as did Krissy's, went straight to voice mail now.

An unanswered cell phone was never a positive sign. Not when a young couple had a kid.

Delilah Merkle skidded to a stop, noticing Tara in the crowd along the counter. "Hey." She made a face. "You look like this isn't about dinner."

During an investigation, Tara never could keep the worry off her face—especially when a child was involved. "Unfortunately, it's not. You're really busy, but we need to talk."

Without hesitation, Delilah motioned for Tara to follow her. Tara kept pace with her along the length of the counter, then cut through at the end and followed her into the space where the magic happened, weaving through the throng of employees in the kitchen. Delilah opened the door to her office, waited for Tara to come inside and then closed the door.

Delilah was the only person Tara knew whose office was always perfectly organized no matter what was going on.

"What's up? The look on your face has me worried." Delilah plopped into the well-worn chair behind her desk, a testament of how exhausted she most certainly was. "Is your dad okay?"

"My dad's good. No new declines." Tara took a breath and launched into what had to be said. "Krissy

Callaway." She hesitated to catch Delilah's reaction prior to sharing the situation.

The long-time diner owner-operator rolled her eyes. "I swear, you'd think I would learn." She threw up her arms. "I hire someone, and they turn out to be great! Always on time. Hardworking. Good with the customers." She shook her head. "I get all happy and certain I have myself a long-term good employee, and what happens? One day they just don't show up. Poof. She really put me in a bind." She gestured to the door behind Tara. "As you can see we're over-whelmed."

There was no easy way to do this. "We have rea-son to believe she's gone missing under suspicious circumstances."

Delilah's frustration faded. "Missing? Are you serious?"

Tara nodded. "She was last seen on Sunday eve-ning around six o'clock, according to her son."

Delilah leaned forward. "What about her hus-band? Jeff?"

"He's missing also."

"Oh, my God." Her hands went to her face, cra-dling her cheeks. "What on earth happened?"

"We don't know yet," Tara admitted. "Had Krissy mentioned any concerns or issues in her personal life? Maybe with her husband or their finances?"

Delilah shook her head with enthusiasm. "They've been doing well. Last year they went through a rough patch financially related to her cancer treatments.

Breast cancer," Delilah explained. "But life has been good for them since. She's been as happy as a clam. I haven't heard the first peep about issues."

Tara managed to repress a flinch at the mention of cancer. "No trouble with her husband?"

"No. They are best friends. Have been since high school. He's always doing sweet things for her. He had the sweetest bouquet and box of chocolates delivered here on Valentine's Day."

Tara thought about the money she'd found under their bed. "You're sure there were no money issues?"

Delilah shrugged. "Not that she mentioned. They were even talking about taking Jacob on a big surprise vacation this summer." Delilah narrowed her gaze and nodded. "During her recovery, Krissy said they had filled out all these forms for help from private donors. I'm thinking someone came through in a big way."

"Did she mention any friends of hers or her husband? Maybe out-of-town friends? Someone who visited recently?"

"Not that I know of."

"Was there anyone here at the diner who socialized with her outside of work? Maybe someone who might have been closer to her?"

Delilah considered the question for a bit. "No one in particular, I don't think. Of course, you're welcome to talk to any of my employees."

"I appreciate that. The sooner we can figure this

out, the sooner we can find Krissy and Jeff. Hopefully safe."

"Look." She shot to her feet. "I'll go out there and relieve them one at a time so they can come talk to you. Will that work?"

"That would be great."

"On it." Delilah rushed around the desk and out the door.

That was one of the things that had brought Tara back to the Hollow. People watched out for each other. People cared. She'd wanted to raise her family here.

Except the family hadn't happened.

She pushed the memory away and prepared for the questions she would need to ask.

One by one, she interviewed the six employees at the diner tonight. They all told the same story. Krissy and Jeff Callaway were very happy. They were a great couple. Hard workers. Good people. Loved their son.

On the way home, Tara checked in with Collin. He'd learned basically the same thing at the hatchery. Both the manager and the shift leader spoke highly of Jeff Callaway. His sudden absence was totally unexpected. He'd been a good employee.

Except for the $50K, Tara mused. All that money hidden in a shoebox under the bed set off all sorts of warning bells.

It was nearly ten by the time Tara rolled up to her

childhood home. Her headlights flashed over an un-expected vehicle. Truck. *Deke's truck*.

Tara parked and turned off the engine. For a moment, she didn't move to get out. She had no energy left for this. All she wanted right now was a long hot shower and a good night's sleep.

If she didn't get out, he would just come over and knock on her window. She climbed out, shut the door and walked toward him. He waited on her porch steps. How long had he been sitting there?

"It's late," she said. "I'm exhausted."

He stood. "Any news?"

He asked this as if she hadn't just given him two perfectly acceptable reasons to climb into his truck and leave.

"Nothing yet." She walked past him and shoved the key into the door lock and twisted. Reached inside and flipped on the porch light. The last thing she wanted was to be in the dark with Deke Shepherd.

"I checked on Jacob a couple hours ago," he said. "He's doing fine for now."

Tara turned back to him, her back to her open door. She would not—could not—let him inside. "Thanks for letting me know. Like I said, I'm beat."

Go. Just please go.

"Should we be worried about Jacob? Is he safe without police protection?"

"At this time, we can't be sure of anything." She had spoken to Brenda Wright about keeping a really close eye on him. She wasn't to allow him outside without supervision. If there was something going on with the parents that was related to the money, Jacob could become a pawn in the game. "Sheriff Decker will be reviewing the situation and making any necessary decisions early tomorrow. The truth is, until we have more information and some sort of evidence, all we know for sure is that the Callaways abandoned their son. Based on Jacob's statement, there's reason to believe their disappearance was under suspicious circumstances. We'll put their photos on the news and on social media. We'll issue BOLOs. Send the info out far and wide to other jurisdictions and hope someone somewhere has seen them. That's really all we can do at this point."

"How are *you* doing?"

She wanted to tell him again that it was late and she was tired, but she knew Deke. He wasn't going anywhere until she forced the issue or he was satisfied with whatever it was he wanted or needed.

"I'm fine. Tired but fine."

"I'm sorry."

Tara took a mental swipe at the exhaustion in hopes of better analyzing his statement. "Sorry for what?"

"I'm sorry for…" He looked away briefly before setting those piercing blue eyes on hers once more. "I'm sorry I couldn't be or do or say whatever you needed. I'm just sorry."

She couldn't take this. Not right now.

"Deke." She held up her hands in a stop-sign fashion. "We don't need to do this." Not again. Not now. She was too tired. Too weak.

He shook his head. "No. You're wrong. I made a mistake six months ago, and I'm not going to keep pretending I'm okay with it." He laughed, a hollow sound. "No matter that I don't have a clue what I did or failed to do, I want to make it right."

Tara closed her eyes a moment before opening them once more and looking him straight in the eye. "Just say what you have to say and get it over with."

"The one thing I did that I wish I hadn't…" He looked away for a moment. "I shouldn't have let you go. I should have helped you face whatever it is you're running from. I should have done something to fix whatever was wrong."

Good grief. She should just tell him—she wasn't fixable.

But she couldn't. Not right now. Maybe not ever.

"Good night, Deke."

She turned her back and escaped into the house. Closed and locked the door and leaned against it, listening to ensure he left.

Deke didn't get it. The thing she was running from was *him*.

Chapter Five

Deke watched his students through the window in the classroom door. Music was a favorite subject for all fifteen students, especially Jacob. His enthusiasm for music, for school in general, was contagious. He had a way of prompting the same from his classmates.

Brenda Wright had caught Deke at the school mail station first thing this morning to tell him about Jacob's nightmares. He'd awakened at two this morning crying out for help. He'd sobbed and shared the painful dream with her. The bad men who'd taken his parents had come back for him. He'd felt torn between wanting to go with them in hopes of seeing his parents and wanting to run for his life in fear.

No child should suffer that level of anxiety.

But in true Jacob form, he'd appeared all smiles in the classroom. Talking and smiling. Deke had struggled with the urge to hug the kid, but the other students wouldn't have understood. Sharing his story with his classmates was something Jacob hadn't done so far.

Deke watched him now, circling around as the group sang the alligator song. Jacob got along with everyone. Interacted well with the entire class. He didn't appear to have a specific or best friend. Just played with anyone who wanted to play.

"Deke."

He started at the sound of his name, particularly since it was Tara who'd said it. "Hey." Worry instantly started its incessant nag. Along with the worry was the complete and utter happiness he always felt at seeing her. "You have some news?"

She glanced at the kids beyond the glass, smiling, laughing, circling around as they sang before she finally met his gaze once more. "Is there somewhere we can talk?"

Whatever news she had, it didn't sound good.

"My classroom will be free for another forty-five minutes. The kids go to lunch from here." He hitched his head toward the music room.

"That'll work."

She started in that direction and he followed. Tara had been to his classroom more than once. She knew the way. She'd spent twelve years of her life in this school. Most of her life in this community. He was the newcomer. Three years wasn't that long compared to the better part of a lifetime.

He was glad she knew the way. Gave him an opportunity to just watch. She was definitely the hottest deputy he'd ever met. Long blonde hair that she kept in a sleek ponytail. The memory of removing that tie and watching all that lush hair fall around her shoulders made him smile.

He blinked away the image and thought of how sharp she always looked in her uniform. Never so much as an errant wrinkle. Shoes always shined. The weight of her utility belt alone should have her moving slow. Not Tara. She was as strong and determined as she was beautiful. Nothing slowed her down.

She'd let him catch her. It was the holding on that had eluded him.

She entered his classroom without pause. He did the same, closing the door behind him. When she finally faced him, he said, "This feels bad."

"It's not good," she confessed. "Jeff Callaway's truck was found this morning."

Deke's hopes fell. "Any sign of Jeff or Kristen?" Everyone called Jacob's mom Krissy, but her name was Kristen.

Tara shook her head. "The CSI folks have taken the truck in to see what they can find, but there was no one and nothing of obvious significance inside. The usual papers and stashes of napkins and drinking straws were found in the glove box and console, but nothing else that tells us the story of what the hell is going on."

Definitely not good.

"Collin and I have scoured their social media pages, not that either parent was particularly active. Their cell phones are with them, so we couldn't check those, though we have requested warrants to get a list of calls and text messages made which, you probably know, takes forever. The phones go straight to voice mail, so it's possible the batteries are down or the phones are turned off. So we know pretty much nothing."

The more she said, the more his hope dwindled.

Tara was one of the first people he'd met three years ago. She'd pulled him over for speeding. He hadn't realized he was speeding. Forty wasn't that fast, but the speed limit along Main Street was thirty-five. She'd insisted she'd let his speeding slide twice already. He had been fairly certain that he'd never met a more gorgeous woman. Blonde hair, green eyes and those lips…

"Deke?"

He blinked. "I'm sorry. What?"

"I was asking when the best time for me to talk to Jacob would be," she said, speaking slowly as if he needed extra time to absorb the words.

He did, actually. She'd had that effect on him from the beginning. He always got lost just looking at her.

"After lunch," he said, kicking himself for going down that path. "We have a short study hall before math class. It gives the kids time to settle down after lunch. You could talk to him then." He smiled at the thought. "You'd be surprised how worked up they get during lunch. Maybe it's the music class this semester or just the fact that it's spring and walking outside from the lunchroom back to the classroom has them ready for something more physical than math."

She smiled. "I imagine so. I remember wanting to cut and run for the playground after lunch."

When they were together, he'd found himself in the school library more than once, going through the old yearbooks to find her. She was beautiful now, and she'd been the cutest little girl with her pigtails and big smiles. He'd wondered if she had been as full of mischief as her expressions suggested. As soon as word got around that they were a couple, some of the older teachers had gone on and on about Tara's escapades back in school. Nothing so bad. Just pranks meant to incite laughter. Never any hurt feelings, just the occasional injured pride. Most times the party with the bruised pride had deserved it. One of her former teachers had referred to Tara and her friend Henry as Robin Hood and a merry bandit for taking down the occasional overblown ego. Sounded exactly like something Tara would do.

He exiled the memories and focused on the now and his mounting concern for Jacob. "Will you tell Jacob what you've found?"

"I don't see any reason to upset him. I'm hoping he will recall if his father drove his truck home last Friday and if the vehicle was still at the house on Sunday. When I questioned him yesterday, he said the two men came to their house and took his par-

ents with them. In that case, Jeff's truck should have
been at home as well—assuming he was there. My
impression was that both parents were home when
the men arrived."

Deke nodded. "That's the impression I got." But
the fact was, Jacob hadn't actually said his father was
home. "He did say that when he came out of hiding
his parents—meaning both—were gone."

She nodded. "He did, but his mother told him to
hide. He didn't mention his father saying anything."

"You think his father wasn't at home? That maybe
he'd been gone because he knew those men were
coming?" The words left a bad taste in Deke's mouth.
What kind of father deserted his family at a time
like that?

"I hope that's not the case," Tara said, on the same
page with him. "Jeff's coworkers stated that he was
a loving father. It's possible the men had already
taken him."

Neither scenario was good, but the latter was more
palatable. "Did the forensic guys find anything at
the house that might tell us who those guys were?"
He caught himself. Shook his head. "I'm sure you
can't share that information." He shrugged. "It's just
Jacob is one of my students and I feel personally involved. With the burglaries, I can't help wondering
if there's a connection."

To his surprise, she smiled instead of setting him
straight on the rules of sharing on one of her cases.
"You are involved. I know how you feel about your

students. That's part of what makes you such a good teacher."

"Thanks." He glanced at the clock above the chalkboard. "You want something from the lounge? There's a drink machine and snack machine."

"No thanks." She made a face that said something had just occurred to her. "This is your planning time. Probably your lunch break too. Don't let me keep you from anything. I can come back in half an hour."

"Stay," he insisted, hoping she actually would. "I'll grab two coffees or two ginger ales—as I recall that's your favorite."

She nodded slowly. "A ginger ale would be good."

He backed toward the door, not taking his gaze off her for fear she might disappear. "I will be right back."

"I'll be right here," she assured him as if she understood he wanted—needed—her to still be in his classroom when he got back.

Deke walked quickly from the elementary wing to the admin hall. The principal's office, school nurse and teachers' lounge as well as the lobby and school store were all in that front wing of the school. The U-shaped building contained the middle school wing on the other side. The upper school classrooms were in a separate building across campus. It was a workable setup that had served the community well for half a century. Deke doubted the school would last many more years. The community wasn't growing, and the number of students dwindled each year. The vote to keep the school open two more years had barely passed.

He wasn't looking forward to moving to a larger institution, but the day would come. There was some talk of a private school purchasing the building and continuing classes here, but Deke wasn't sure how many students in the community would be able to afford a private school. The influx of parents, even if only to drop off and pick up their kids, would likely supplement the local economy, but it would also change things. Deke had gotten used to the sleepy little town and knowing life would be calm and quiet most of the time. The recent surge in break-ins notwithstanding.

Things changed. No way to get around the reality that nothing stayed the same.

Like relationships.

The lounge was empty, preventing him from having to explain why Deputy Norwood was here to see him. That was one downside—sort of—to small community living. News traveled at hyper speed. Everyone knew everything about each other. He poked money into the machine and made his first selection. The idea wasn't entirely true. Otherwise Jacob's parents wouldn't be missing without someone knowing something, right?

He added more cash and tapped the necessary image for a second ginger ale. The idea nagged at him. Really, how could the Callaways live in the Hollow—for, what, two and a half years?—and not have anyone close enough to have some clue what was happening with them?

Inspired now, Deke grabbed the two cans and hurried back to his classroom. He hesitated at the door. Tara stood at the bulletin board, studying the items posted there. For the past three weeks, he'd posted a different board every day. Each board a story about a student. These kids would move on to fourth grade together. The school had only one class at each grade level. He wanted the students to better understand each other, so he'd given the assignment to the kids and their parents. Create your story. The students would bring photos of their parents and siblings as well as of themselves. The story boards included their favorite foods and vacation spots, what their parents did at their jobs, what they wanted to do when they grew up and who their heroes were. All fifteen chose a parent or grandparent for a hero. When each story board went up, the other students were asked to provide one nice word each about that student to add to the board. The story boards had been a hit with the students as well as the parents.

The board Tara stared at now was Deke's. The class had insisted that he do one as well. He hadn't expected Tara to be in his classroom or maybe he wouldn't have been so totally honest on one particular point.

He opened the door and walked in. Her gaze, clearly startled, swung toward him as if she'd completely forgotten he would be returning.

"Don't judge me," he said as he extended a can of ginger ale.

"Homemade tacos are your favorite food?" She took the can and popped the top.

He did the same. "You got me hooked on home-made ones. I haven't been able to look at a fast-food taco the same since."

She laughed, almost choked on her drink. She pressed her hand to her lips. "I'm not a great cook."

"But you make great tacos."

The blush that settled high on her cheeks made him smile. "Maybe so," she agreed.

He walked to the board. "Do you like my hero?" He'd posted a photo of her as the person he consid-ered to be a hero. And now she knew.

She nodded, her smile fading. "I'm not a hero, Deke."

He held her gaze, wishing he could see beyond those shimmering green eyes to what she was think-ing. "You're the person I use as an example when I talk to the kids about who they can trust if they need help. They all know you. Just another perk of life in a small community."

Tara looked away, downed another swallow of her drink. She cleared her throat and said, "I know at least three women in this little community who would love to get to know you better." She looked directly at him then. "You're a great catch, Deke. You shouldn't be holding yourself back."

He was. Holding himself back. He'd had invita-

tions during the past six months. Enough to be flat-
tered. From really nice women. But he couldn't say
yes. He refused to mislead anyone. The last thing he
wanted to do was to hurt another person. He'd been
down that road. Loving someone who couldn't or
wouldn't love him back. He refused to be the reason anyone took that journey. Ever. He wasn't a two-
out-of-three kind of guy. Part of him wondered if the
reason Tara had pushed him away was that her feelings just hadn't gone as deep as his. But he couldn't
see that. He knew what he felt, what he felt in her.

"You know my story better than anyone in the
Hollow, Tara. How can you expect me to do anything different than what I'm doing?"

She turned away, walked to the wall of windows
that overlooked the courtyard between the elementary and middle school wings.

"I told you up front I wasn't what you were looking for."

This was true. She hadn't minced words. She had
been divorced for just over two years at the time, and
she had insisted there would be no going back to
that status. She was done. Deke had found the idea
foolish. She was two years younger than him. Who
gave up on marriage and a family at thirty-two? She
was only thirty-three now. She had her whole life
ahead of her.

He joined her at the windows. Watched his class
march across the courtyard toward the cafeteria. The
truth was he wanted children. As much as he adored

the students in his class, he wanted a family of his own. It wasn't until he made this admission to Tara that their relationship had changed. She'd pulled back. Three weeks later, they were done—her words.

Deke had gone over those last couple of months a thousand times. He couldn't put his finger on a single other thing that had changed. They shared a love of hiking, of dogs, of life in general. They were happy, or so he'd thought. She had loved him. He knew it when he saw it, experienced it. He'd been in love before and he'd had someone who loved him before. There was no mistaking the feeling. No mistaking the look in your partner's eyes. Tara had loved him.

"You were wrong." He said this without looking at her. She certainly wouldn't look at him now.

She drew in a deep breath. "I have some calls to make. I'll be back in thirty to talk to Jacob."

He watched her walk out without a backward glance...without the slightest hesitation.

She was wrong. He wasn't sure what it would take to make her see just how wrong she was, but he intended to wait.

He had time.

Speaking of time, she waited the full half hour before returning. The kids were back and having quiet study time.

When he saw her at the door, he walked to Jacob's desk and tapped him on the shoulder. Since he'd already given Jacob a heads-up, he was prepared. He left the classroom without anyone else paying any real attention. Deke stepped into the corridor with him.

"Jacob, I'm sorry to bother you at school," Tara said. She kept her attention on the student and didn't spare Deke a glance.

He always ended up pushing too hard.

Apparently, he hadn't learned his lesson yet.

"I don't mind," Jacob said. "I like talking to you."

Deke smiled, grateful Tara had so easily earned the boy's trust. This was a very difficult time for him. He needed people he trusted around him.

Tara smiled and it took Deke's breath. "I'm glad. I have just a couple of questions."

He nodded his understanding.

"When the men came to your house on Sunday, was your father home or was it just you and your mom?"

He shook his head. "My dad had gone to the store. We were out of milk and he needed gas for the work week."

"So it was just you and your mom."

He nodded his agreement. "Wait. At first. Then my dad came home. But everything happened so fast then. Those men were already outside. I guess they saw my dad, and that's when they decided to come in."

"Your mom ushered you into hiding and went to the door."

"My mama and dad both told me to hide. My dad put me in the closet."

"So when your parents left you hidden in your room, what happened then?" She shrugged. "Did you hear your father say anything in particular to the men?"

"I could hear his voice. He was yelling, but I couldn't understand what he was saying." He made a face. "It happened really fast. I mean it felt like forever, but it wasn't long, really. They came in, shouting at my mom. She started shouting too, except her voice wasn't, like, angry." His face fell. "She sounded scared. Like it did that time when I fell out of the tree and broke my collar bone."

Last fall. Deke recalled the incident. Jacob had been out of school for a few days. When he'd returned, the entire class had reveled in hearing the story of how he tried to hang on to a branch after falling part way but lost his grip and hit the ground. His vivid descriptions had enthralled them all.

Tara nodded. "Good. Thank you for clearing that up. One more thing, had your parents mentioned moving?"

Jacob shook his head no. "They did tell me we were going on a special vacation this year. They wouldn't tell me where, but I think I know." He grinned. "I've always wanted to go." He glanced around and lowered his voice. "I think it's in Florida."

Deke hoped like hell that vacation still happened for the kid. It made him sick to think that his life as he knew it might be over.

"Wow," Tara said. "That sounds awesome. I'm

sure you'll have a blast. Did your parents ever talk or argue about money?"

She'd asked this question yesterday. Deke had a feeling she knew or suspected something was up with the family finances.

"Not since last year when Mom was sick." The remembered worry on his face was impossible to miss. "She's all better now and there's no money troubles. She told me just the other day that they would never have to worry about money again."

Tara nodded. "Thank you, Jacob. You're really a big help. I know your parents would be proud."

A big smile slid across his face. "I hope you find them soon."

Tara nodded but didn't make any promises this time.

"Go back to your desk now," Deke told him. When the kid was back in the classroom, he asked, "You think his parents were involved in something that put them in danger?"

She moistened her lips. "Unfortunately, yes. But for now, it's only a hunch."

"Damn." He shook his head. "I don't get how anyone could do something like that when there's a kid involved."

"I can only assume there are things we don't know. Whatever the motive," Tara offered, "it must have felt worth the risk."

Deke got that. There were some things that were worth any risk.

He reached out, couldn't stop himself, and touched her hand. The connection was instant and fierce. Always was. She drew away from his reach just as quickly.

"Thanks for putting up with my interruptions," she said, preparing to escape.

Whenever they saw each other and he attempted any sort of interaction, this is what she did. If not for this case, she would have steered wide and clear of him.

"Whatever you need. I'm happy to help in any way I can."

She flashed a smile that fell sorely short of the ones that so easily stole his breath. "See ya."

She walked away, her steps bordering on a run.

Could he be that wrong about what he'd felt for her?

Maybe it was time he gave real consideration to the idea that she didn't feel and never had felt the way he did.

When she solved this case, she would go back to avoiding him at all costs again. He made up his mind then and there. Until then, he intended to do all in his power to figure out what was and what wasn't real.

Equally important, he intended to figure out how to live with whatever he found.

Chapter Six

Sergeant Darrell Snelling of the Hamilton County Sheriff's Department CSI team had asked to meet Tara at two at the Callaway residence. She checked the time. He would be here soon. She hoped he'd found something significant that would help her find Jacob's parents.

Collin had reinterviewed the neighbors on Valley Drive. No one had seen or heard anything. Most hadn't been home on Sunday evening. Spring brought all sorts of festivals in surrounding communities. On top of that, many churches held evening services on Sunday. None of the neighbors had security cameras, not even the doorbell type. Three more of the father's coworkers had been interviewed, and none could provide any helpful input. Tara had spoken with the mother's coworkers and none were aware of any trouble in the Callaway family.

The best explanation in Tara's opinion was that

whatever had prompted the disappearance was new. There hadn't been time to share the details with even the closest of their friends.

Tara had worked a couple of missing persons cases before moving to the Hollow. Both had ended well, but she wouldn't call herself experienced. Or even particularly skilled in the area. To complicate matters further, there was a serious shortage of deputies and officers in Hamilton County, leaving no extra bodies to share.

She and Collin were on their own unless some aspect of the case that had not been ferreted out or had not presented itself as of yet fell under the FBI's jurisdiction. Although she hated to lose control of a case, if the feds could help find Jacob's parents, she was only too happy to hand it over.

A sedan carrying the CSI logo came to a stop nose to nose with Tara's Wagoneer. She was about to find out what they had. She climbed out of her vehicle and met Snelling on the street. The sergeant was a big man. Six-three or six-four. Broad shoulders. Huge hands. His black hair was peppered with gray. Sunglasses shielded his eyes. His neatly pressed shirt and trousers looked right out of the dry cleaner.

"Deputy Norwood." He gave her a nod and extended his hand.

Tara accepted the gesture. "I'm hoping you've found something that will provide some forward momentum for my investigation."

"Let's step inside."

She ducked under the perimeter crime-scene tape and led the way to the front door. Snelling unlocked the door and sliced the tape that marked the house as off-limits to anyone not on the CSI team.

They didn't bother donning gloves or shoe covers since the team had completed its work inside.

"I found a loose floorboard under one of the beds."

He led the way through the house and, to Tara's surprise, into Jacob's room. The twin-size bed had been set aside and the small Spider-Man character rug covering the hardwood floor rolled back.

"There's a compartment built between the floor joists," Snelling explained.

Tara knelt down and inspected the compartment. Two pieces of flooring, measuring about fourteen inches long and four inches wide each, lifted from the top of the compartment. When in place, it was hardly noticeable that they weren't connected to the rest of the flooring. The compartment was somewhat longer and wider than the combined floorboards.

"Was there anything inside?" She got back to her feet, dusted off her hands.

"Twenty-five hundred dollars and a few prints. Based on prints we lifted from toothbrushes and other personal items, we believe they belong to Jeff Callaway."

Damn. "Twenty-five hundred dollars? So maybe this was his hiding place. The couple have a joint checking account but no savings account." This was a reasonable amount of money the couple could have saved from their work.

"Possibly," Snelling agreed. "We didn't find the wife's prints on the money or in and around the hiding place."

"What about the shoebox and the money in it?"

"Again, the husband's, but not the wife's."

Tara felt some amount of relief. Still, just because Jacob's mother hadn't handled the money didn't mean she wasn't involved in however it ended up in the home.

"There's something else."

Tara held her breath, hoped for something useful in finding Krissy and Jeff Callaway. Whatever they had gotten themselves involved in, they obviously needed help and Jacob needed them.

"We recovered a number of other prints from the cash in the shoebox," he went on. "Do you remember hearing about the Treat Foster case?"

"It doesn't ring a bell." Tara silently repeated the name in an attempt to dredge something from her memory bank.

"It's an old case. About thirty years back, I think. Treat Foster stole five hundred thousand dollars from a Chattanooga bank where he served as president. He was never found. He just disappeared with the money. His ex-wife couldn't figure out what happened to him. He just went into the bank one day, took the money and left, never to be seen again. Some said it was because his wife had left him for his former best friend. They had no kids, so walking away from his life was only about his career. Whatever the case, he was never seen or heard from again."

"Unbelievable." All that he'd just told her suddenly bloomed big in her brain. "Are you saying part of the five hundred thousand dollars was in that shoebox under the Callaway's bed?"

He nodded. "The FBI has already reached out. As soon as those prints hit the system, I got a call. Special Agent James Hanson is heading this way. I gave him your name and number."

"Got it, but this is a little out there. The Callaways are my age," she argued, mostly with herself. "They couldn't have been involved with Foster."

Snelling shrugged. "Beats me. I can only tell you the facts."

"What about the secret compartment?" She glanced down at the hole in the floor. "Maybe a former tenant put the money there. Surely there were other prints on the cash or inside the compartment."

"None that came up in the system, but I can tell you the compartment is fairly new." He reached down and picked up one of the two pieces of flooring. "See the cut end."

He was right. She got it. "The cut is recent." Once wood was cut, the new clean edge started to age. It took time for the fresh edge to darken.

He nodded. "The plywood used to make the compartment is new too. You can still smell the cuts made to size the pieces."

Whatever Tara had expected or hoped for, this was not it.

"Anything else I should know before I plow through the reports?"

He shook his head. "The place was clean beyond the cash. That said, we can't release the scene until Agent Hanson has a look. He may be sending his own forensic team."

"Thanks for all your hard work, Sergeant Snelling."

"I wish I'd been able to give you some answers rather than more questions."

"Just makes me have to earn my pay." She smiled. "I had a feeling this case was not going to be easy by any definition of the word."

As they exited the house, Snelling said, "You should talk to your father. He was a brand-new sheriff at the time. He may recall more about the case." Snelling seemed to catch himself. "Oh, hell. I forgot about—"

"No worries," she assured him. "I forget sometimes too. I will ask him though. He seems to be able to remember more about the past than about the present."

Tara sat in her Wagoneer for a bit after Snelling drove away. She should drop by Forrest Hills. Ask her father about the case. It would make him happy to talk about work. He'd spent twenty-five years as sheriff. There was a lot he knew about Hamilton County, particularly Dread Hollow. He should know plenty about the Hollow. He'd grown up here. Was a fourth-generation Norwood in the area.

She started her vehicle and headed in that direction. When her father had entered Forrest Hills, he had been diagnosed as in the second stage of Alzheimer's disease. Nothing Tara had said would change his mind about moving into the facility. They had a special wing for Alzheimer's patients, and when he reached the next stage he would be moving into that wing. For now, he was on the assisted-living side. He had a reasonable level of freedom. But that would change soon enough.

Tara parked and made her way into the posh facility. She had to give her father credit, he had great taste.

She checked in at the front desk or what Forrest Hills called the concierge's counter. The attractive concierge on duty told Tara that her father was in his room. Since the last escape, they'd placed monitor bracelets on all the residents. A system monitored their positions at all times.

Beyond the large windows lining the walls, older folks milled around the beautifully landscaped property. The lounge was full of card players and those tucked away in reading nooks. No doubt it was a classy place. Comfortable and with all sorts of very nice amenities. Lots of other folks her father's age. But it wasn't home, and she wished her father were home.

She knocked at his door. He announced, "Come on in, Tara."

This was another update. Residents were notified when visitors arrived on the property. She opened the door and couldn't help smiling. Her father was hunched over his portable worktable, occupied with the creation of one of his models. He loved vintage sports cars. Since he no longer drove or owned one, he enjoyed working with the models.

"Hey, Dad." She leaned down and gave him a kiss on the cheek. "You feeling okay today?"

Tarrence Norwood set his tools aside and removed his loupe lenses before flashing her a broad smile. "I'm above ground. That's always a good thing, and I feel fine. The real question is can I remember if I took my meds or where I am."

"Well," she settled on the comfy sofa, "can you?"

"I can. Any time I can do that I consider it a good day."

Even at seventy the man was still incredibly handsome. She didn't understand why he'd never married again after her mother's death. Certainly not for lack of opportunity.

"And how is my favorite daughter?"

"I'm good and your only daughter, by the way."

He grinned. "I know that."

"We had a couple go missing over the weekend, and you're never going to believe what popped up in the case."

He stood, stretched his back, swaggered over to the sofa and sat down on the other end. "Don't keep me in suspense, girl. Spit it out."

"In the home of the missing couple, we found a

secret compartment in the floor, which in and of it-self isn't a big deal. These days, folks like to tuck things away where thieves can't find them."

"Like guns and drugs and such," he offered.

She nodded. "We found twenty-five hundred dollars in there." She shrugged. "No big surprise considering the couple work and maybe they've saved. But we also found fifty thousand dollars in cash in a shoebox under the bed."

"Seems strange the $50K wasn't in the secret compartment."

"Agreed," she said. "Maybe they'd only recently come into possession of it, and there had been no time."

"Sounds to me," he said, "like they were involved in one of the trades."

Tara knew what he meant. "Drugs, guns or human trafficking."

He nodded. "We try to keep our communities free of that kind of activity, but sometimes they slip in. By the way, what's up with all these burglaries lately? All the old-timers around here are talking about it."

"Collin and I are still working on that one," she admitted. "There's no pattern to their targets or their hits."

"Hmm," he grunted. "Sounds like teenagers to me."

"It does. They know their way in and out of the houses. Has to be local. There doesn't seem to be any planning either. They go in, get the first marketable items they see and they're gone. Several of the houses have had far more valuable items in the bedrooms, but they never seem to get past the living room."

Her father shook his head. "Kids, I'm telling you. So what about the money and the missing couple? Any connection to these snatch and runners?"

"Not that we've found. We don't know yet how the couple came into possession of the money, but we do know where the money came from before they had it. Way before, in fact."

His forehead pleated in confusion. "You've lost me."

"The Treat Foster case. The missing half a mil. The fifty thousand was part of that stolen cash."

He perked up, eyes wide. "Are you serious?"

"I am."

"I had just stepped into the sheriff's position when Foster disappeared with that money."

"Snelling told me to talk to you. He remembered the case."

"It was a bizarre mystery, to say the least."

"I'd love to hear whatever you can recall."

He rubbed at his stubbled chin. She'd been surprised the first time she saw him wearing two-day-old stubble. He'd promptly informed her that he'd spent fifty-odd years shaving every morning; now he shaved when he wanted to. She couldn't argue with his reasoning.

"Treat Foster was president of the First Community downtown. He was a deacon at his church. Married more than half his life. Never so much as had a parking ticket. One day he just walked into the bank, packed up $500K and walked out. Wife, friends, co-workers, no one had a clue where he'd gone or why he'd done such a thing."

"Did you know him personally?"

"In passing," he admitted. "He and his family attended the same church as your mother and me, just at different locations. There were times when special events brought us to the same house of God. So yes, we were acquainted."

"Any ideas on how this money ended up in the Hollow?"

He shook his head. "I can't think of a single reason. But if something comes to me, I'll let you know." His frown deepened. "This couple who's gone missing, are they originally from the Hollow?"

"No, they moved here year before last. They came up from Florida."

"Maybe they brought the money with them." He shrugged. "If I had been Foster, I would have headed south. Maybe a little farther than Florida."

"I don't think they brought the money with them." Tara considered what she had learned from their co-workers. "Krissy, the wife, had breast cancer last year. The financial burden was tremendous. They had a really hard time. Those closest to her said things had turned around the past few months. It feels more like a recent windfall."

"I'd say there's your answer. You find out where

that windfall came from, and the rest will fall into place."

"The simplest answer is usually the right one," she said, repeating the words of wisdom she'd heard from him a thousand times.

"Exactly." His face formed a hopeful look. "Have you talked to Deke lately? He dropped by for a visit the other day." The frown reappeared. "Might have been on Sunday. I can't recall."

Her father had always been able to hang on to the smallest detail. The idea of losing that ability and so much more had to be killing him.

"Deke visited? That was nice of him."

"He visits every couple of weeks," her father said. "I'm sure I've told you this."

He hadn't, but she held any comment.

"He misses you." Her father's face softened. "You should talk to him, Tara. Work things out."

She shot to her feet. "I should go. I have to meet that FBI guy." She gave her dad a hug. "Thanks, Dad. You call me if you think of anything about Foster's case that might be relevant to my missing couple."

"You got it. Think about what I said," he called after her as she left.

She hated to cut and run this way, but she had no desire to talk about Deke with anyone, not even her father.

As she drove away from Forrest Hills, she couldn't help feeling wistful. Her father was her last living relative. When he was gone, she would be all alone.

The thought occurred to her all too often these days. Her mother had been an only child. Her father's only brother had been a casualty of war. Not a single living relative. At least not one that she knew.

The idea immediately summoned Deke's image despite her best efforts.

She dismissed the visual. He was not the answer. There were far more things to consider than just her loneliness. She would not transfer her problem onto someone else just to prevent being alone in the world. It wouldn't be fair.

She wouldn't do that to Deke. He didn't understand her reasoning because she couldn't bring herself to tell him her secret.

If she did, he would only insist that it didn't matter and force the issue of them getting back together. She could not allow that to happen. It wouldn't be right.

When she arrived at the substation, a black sedan sat in the small parking area. Judging by the license plate, most likely the federal agent, Hanson.

She climbed out of her Wagoneer and walked into the office. A man wearing a stylish suit and perfect hair waited. He turned to her, hands on hips.

"Deputy Norwood, I presume."

Deep voice. Classic features. Late thirties, early forties maybe. Clearly he had inherited the cold case.

"Agent Hanson?"

"I see you got word I was coming."

"I did."

"You have some time for me now?"

She resisted the urge to ask if it mattered. He was here. It wasn't like she was going to say no. "Sure. Come on into my office."

Her office was small, but there was an extra chair for the occasional visitor.

They had just taken their seats when Tara found her manners. "Can I get you a bottle of water or a soft drink?"

"No thanks. I'm good."

"Where would you like to begin?"

"Snelling met me at the crime scene and showed me around. What I really need from you at this point is whatever you can tell me about the missing couple."

"Not that much. They moved to the Hollow year before last. Husband works at the hatchery. Wife works at the local diner. Their son, nine, attends the elementary school. No domestic issues. No criminal connections or record of any sort. There was a medical and financial crisis last year. At this time and considering the financial issues, I'm leaning toward the idea that the family was desperate and made a bad decision and it hasn't gone well from there."

"I'd like a list of the coworkers, family and friends you've interviewed."

"There is no family, other than their son, Jacob. I can ready those lists for you right now if you don't mind waiting."

"That would be perfect."

Tara pulled a notepad toward her. "If you'll share

your contact info, it'll be easier to pass along information as it comes in."

"Sure." He reached into an interior pocket and produced a business card.

"Thanks." Tara entered his number into her phone. When they had first started working together Collin laughed at her when she said if her phone didn't tell her to do it, she didn't. But she was dead serious. It was her calendar and her alarm clock, her reminder list and more.

When she'd completed the list, she passed it to the federal agent.

Hanson looked it over, then stood. "I have to get back to the city. I look forward to hearing from you with any additional details."

Tara stood, wishing she had more already. "I'd appreciate anything useful you can share that might help my case as well."

He was at the exit, she'd followed, before he hesitated. "There is one thing you might find interesting, though we were never able to make the connection."

"I'll take anything I can get."

"For an entire year before he disappeared, Foster took one afternoon off each week and made a trip that his wife and employees never understood when they learned about the outings after his death."

"Trip?"

"He drove to your little community, Deputy. Spent a few hours and then went home. No one seems to have any idea why he came here or who he saw—if anyone. However, this is our first solid evidence of his presence here in all this time."

Just her luck.

She had her first missing persons case in the Hollow, and it was connected to a decades-old cold case of another missing person.

And half a million bucks.

Chapter Seven

Lake Trail, 7:45 p.m.

Tara took a deep breath, raised her fist and knocked on the door.

She had struggled with this decision for the better part of an hour. Then she'd done what deep down she knew she had to do.

The door opened and Deke stood there, staring at her as if an alien had landed in his front yard and was now at his door.

"Tara? Is everything all right?"

Of course he would be shocked. She hadn't been here—at his home—in nearly six months. She'd sworn to herself she would never come back. Couldn't. Going back would be a mistake—one she refused to make.

She swallowed back the big lump in her throat—her pride most likely. "Do you have a few minutes? I wanted to ask a favor of you."

He visibly shook himself as if throwing off the shock of her appearance. "Come in. Please."

Bracing herself, she stepped over the threshold. The scent of something delicious filled her lungs. She cringed. "I'm sorry, I'm interrupting your evening."

He grinned. "No way. I like to cook and you know I always cook too much. You're here, you might as well join me. It'll be ready in about fifteen minutes."

She shook her head so hard it hurt. "No, I couldn't—"

"Tara," he interrupted, "you're here. I'll wager you haven't had dinner. It won't kill you to share a meal with me."

He had no idea.

"If you insist." Surrendering was easier than she'd expected. Probably not a good sign. Maybe the whole alone in the world idea looming over her was getting under her skin.

He closed the door and motioned for her to follow him to the kitchen. She did. Not that she needed a guide. She knew this house inside out. Had spent way more time here than she had at home during their five-month-and-twenty-day relationship.

Why could she not get the dates out of her head? It was like some sort of obsession.

They had now officially been apart longer than they had been together. By a couple of days anyway. Not that she was keeping track or anything. Giving herself grace, she had broken things off on her birthday. It wasn't like she could forget that day.

Perfect explanation. She wasn't obsessing. Not at all.

Deke returned to the stove and busied himself stirring pots. Smelled like his homemade spaghetti sauce.

As if she'd said the words aloud, he flashed her a smile. "It's impossible to cook spaghetti for one person."

She nodded, made an attempt at a smile that felt brittle at best.

"Make yourself at home," he said with a nod toward the table. "Water, wine and beer are in the fridge. What's your pleasure?"

To truly answer that question would not be a smart move.

She shuffled to the counter where the bottle of wine waited and opened it. Water wouldn't make the cut. She selected a glass from the cupboard and poured a hefty serving, then made her way to the table. Downed a long swallow and sat down though she felt vastly uncomfortable, particularly since she was out of uniform.

After her meeting with Agent Hanson, she'd gone home, showered and changed into jeans and a tee. She'd planned to relax and consider where to go with the investigation. That had always been her way— her dad's too. She had even poured a glass of wine and sat with her notepad and pen handy to brainstorm possibilities.

Collin had called and they'd discussed the day's findings. It had been during their conversation that she'd come up with the idea of talking to Deke. It had seemed like a really good idea at that moment. She'd even mentioned it to Collin and he had agreed. Now, sitting in Deke's kitchen watching him at the stove, it felt like a really bad idea.

It would certainly have been easier if she'd still been wearing her uniform. The armor of work attire helped considerably when faced with a too personal situation. She turned her head away from him and stared out the window over the sink. She'd always liked his cottage. The three cottages on Lake Trail were all built of stone with views of the small lake and cloaked by woods. This time of year, the area was particularly gorgeous with all the blooming trees. Dogwoods, redbuds. Lots of lovely whites and pinkish purples. Forsythias splashed yellow around the yards. It was nice.

Like the man.

Her gaze wandered back to Deke, who was busy plating the meal he'd prepared.

She closed her eyes and forced away the deluge of memories of moments exactly like this one. Him cooking dinner and teasing her with taste tests. He really was an amazing cook. An amazing teacher. An amazing man. Amazing lover. She swallowed hard. Fought the urge to watch his movements.

No need to torture yourself. She drank more of her wine instead.

He appeared at the table with two steaming plates. "Here we go."

The plates settled on the table. "You want a re-fill?" He backed toward the waiting bottle.

"I'll take water this time." Her throat felt incredibly dry.

He grabbed a water for her, poured himself a glass of wine and joined her at the table. She opened her mouth to start her questions, but he held up a hand. "Eat while it's hot."

She focused on her plate and ate. The sauce fired across her taste buds and she had to suppress a moan. God, she missed this.

She swallowed. Almost choked.

Stop. Just stop.

Forcing her mind to other things, she considered the pleasant layout of the cottage. All the cottages were small, two bed, one bath. The living room was good sized, but more floor space had been allotted to the kitchen, which was actually a combination kitchen and dining room. No bar or island, just a big table and chairs in the center. Lots of windows, the casement type that opened out instead of sliding up and down, lending a storybook look and feel.

Deke had bought his cottage fully furnished. The former owner had passed with no remaining family, so the furnishings had been sold with the house. According to the deceased's will, the proceeds would be donated to creating a small library for Dread Hollow. The library was up and running last year. Delilah had owned a small shop just off Main Street that once held a candy store. She'd donated the small space for the library, which left enough money for the reno, the stocking of books and a part-time librarian's salary for a few years.

Folks in Dread Hollow came together that way. The community was nothing like its name, which was based on the legend of hauntings at Ruby Falls. The haunted house named after Dread Hollow was famous, but their community not so much, beyond the big annual Halloween festival.

Her father always said that the Hollow would have withered up and died long ago if not for the haunted house. Tara supposed that was true.

She blinked, recalling something else her father had said. "You visit my father?"

Deke sat his fork aside. "I do."

She hadn't meant for the question to come out like an accusation, but there it was.

"Do you mind?" he asked when she said nothing for a beat or so.

"Sorry. No, of course not. I was just surprised, that's all."

He shrugged, took a swallow of his wine. He was usually a beer drinker. She preferred wine. Was the wine left over from their couple days? Or maybe he was seeing someone else.

Surprise or something like that flared through her. She'd told him to move on numerous times, but she hadn't actually visualized it.

How thoughtless and selfish of her.

How incredibly difficult that would be to watch.

"I was friends with your father before *us*," he reminded her.

The game. Oh yes, she remembered. "The chess games."

How had she forgotten? The two had met once a week to play chess. When Deke moved to the Hollow, he'd asked Delilah if there was anyone who played chess. Tara's father had been looking for what he called a "victim" for ages. Since his old friend, who used to be the principal of the school, had moved to Florida.

"I drop by every other Sunday to play. He seems to really enjoy it."

Her heart squeezed. "That's very nice of you."

"Nice?" He shook his head. "Nice has nothing to do with it. I'm still trying to beat him."

She laughed. "He's very, very good at the game."

"Indeed," Deke agreed. "You may have noticed the secretary desk in the living room of his apartment."

Tara nodded. "It was my mother's favorite piece."

"Inside is the chessboard. When I arrive, he opens the cabinet and slides the board forward. We pull up our chairs and start to play. It's the perfect setup."

She thought of the two wood chairs, also antiques, standing on either side of the large secretary. The apartment wasn't that large, so her father had found a way to organize the small place to suit his interests.

"Where there's a will, there's a way." And her father certainly had a hell of a will.

"You wanted to ask a favor?"

Tara pushed aside all the tender thoughts associated with her father and what used to be and explained the seeming Trent Foster connection to Jacob's missing parents. Even now, after discussing it with Snelling, Hanson and her father, it seemed surreal.

"That's incredible." Deke gave his head a shake as if to dislodge the surprise. "I remember seeing something about the Foster case on some true crime show years ago. How do you plan to proceed with investigating that aspect? Sounds like a shot in the dark at best."

"Since we have no proof of any connection to Foster here in the Hollow, then we dig. Talk to people. Obviously if there was any information to be found online, the FBI would have it. In this case, any connection—if it actually exists—will have to be found the old-fashioned way. Pounding the pavement, so to speak."

"What can I do to help?"

"The Hollow might be small, but it's spread out, and people who lived here thirty years ago and might remember the case could all be gone now."

"Passed away or moved away," he suggested.

"Right. The hope is if we learn about someone who knew him, that a friend or relative of that person is still here. The easiest way to ensure we don't miss any opportunities is to talk to people who are most connected to the community and solicit their help in the search. Like Delilah. Running the diner for so many years, she knows most everyone."

Deke nodded. "You want me to talk to people at the school."

"Yes. Teachers, assistants, bus drivers, anyone and everyone. Foster spent his weekly visits here somewhere, presumably with someone."

Deke considered her request for a moment. "I can do that. On one condition."

Frustration welled instantly. "Deke, this isn't the time—"

"You allow me to be a part," he explained, cutting her off, "of the investigation."

"What does that mean? A part? This is an official investigation. We can't have someone who isn't a member of the department involved. There could be legal issues with information and evidence. There are rules, Deke."

He held up both hands. "I don't mean like that. I'm merely asking you to use me as a sounding board. Allow me to throw out possibilities. You know, brainstorm together."

She understood what he was asking. His goal was for them to spend time together. "Deke, how can I make this any clearer? We are not a couple anymore."

"But," he argued, undeterred, "we are friends."

This was a mistake. She had recognized the error before she made it. But she made it anyway.

"You're right. We are friends. Your help will be greatly appreciated. I would be happy to brainstorm with you." Truth was Collin had a wife and three kids. It was tough to find extra time with him for brainstorming.

"We can start now, if you'd like," he offered.

The excitement in his eyes and in that deep voice of his made her chest ache. "Sure. That would be great."

He stood. "I'll grab a couple of notepads and pens."

She nodded. "I'll clean up in here."

He argued with her about the cleanup, but she won that round. When he offered to help, she ushered him away. She knew this kitchen as well as her own. During their time as a couple, Deke had been the cook and she'd taken cleanup detail. Being the gentleman he was, he had always insisted on helping with the cleanup. The memory of laughing as she washed and he dried echoed in her mind.

This was a mistake, but somehow she couldn't stop herself from barreling forward.

When she finished up in the kitchen, Deke had started a fire. It was unseasonably cool tonight. The stone fireplace, with its ancient beam for a mantle, was particularly lovely with even a small fire blazing. Notepads and pens lay on the coffee table next to the open bottle of red and the vintage stemware they'd found at an antique shop in old-town Chattanooga.

Tara drew in a deep breath and took the dive. He settled on the sofa. In the past, she would have joined him there. Instead, she took the chair on the opposite side of the table. She picked up her wine glass and leaned back in her chair.

"Merrilee Bryant would be a good person to start with," she said of the cafeteria manager. "She's worked at the school for fifty years. I'm certain she knows every single person who has lived in the Hollow during that time."

Tara might be in precarious territory, but she intended to stay on task.

Deke wrote the name down on one of the pads. "How about Geneva Edmonton? She's been around a while too."

"Good idea." Edmonton was the secretary in the principal's office. She'd outlived three principals and four husbands. There was little she didn't know about the Hollow. "She'll be happy to tell her life story to you."

He laughed. "I'm certain she will. Even at seventy-eight, she gets around."

Tara smiled. "I heard she's dating Claude Watson since his wife passed."

Deke shrugged. "There aren't that many eligible bachelors in the Hollow."

"Everyone deserves to be happy," Tara said without thinking. "Who says there's a time limit or a set number of times allowed for that kind of happiness?"

The question was a rhetorical one. A thought foolishly spoken aloud.

Deke said nothing. Focused on the notepad and the two names there.

She was glad he'd decided not to call her on that one. Because her decision wasn't about her happiness. It was about his. He just didn't know it.

"Ralph Baker," he said as he wrote down the name.

"Right," Tara said following his line of thinking. "Mr. Baker teaches that financial literacy class to sophomores. I remember that class. He went really in-depth about banking."

"He's the right age," Deke pointed out. "A lifelong resident of the Hollow."

"And he knows everything about banking," she agreed. "Even if he hadn't known Foster personally, he will remember the case."

"He'll also remember if he ever saw him around town." Deke looked at her hopefully.

"No question."

This was good, she decided. Really good.

"What about Seth Harbinger?" she asked. "He teaches journalism to the juniors. I would imagine he has always kept his finger on the pulse of breaking news. Back when we had a small newspaper, he often contributed."

"He's the right age." Deke added Harbinger to the list.

Tara's mind skipped to Jacob. "Do you know if there is anyone listed as an emergency contact for Jacob besides his parents?"

"I don't remember anyone else, but I can check in the morning."

"If the parents have family even in another state,

they may have shared something with them that could help with the investigation." None of the co-workers interviewed recalled distant relatives.

"I can talk to Jacob also," Deke offered, "even if there's no one listed."

Tara had planned to do so, but it would be less stressful coming from Deke. "I would appreciate that. As much as I feel I built trust with Jacob, the less often I can disrupt his life, the better. I'm a reminder that his family is missing and haven't been found yet."

Deke let go a burdened breath. "He had nightmares last night. I talked to him. He feels like he should have helped his parents rather than stayed hidden while the bad men took them."

"No. He did exactly what he should have." Tara shook her head, the news making her feel worse. "I hope you explained to him that his staying safe was the best thing he could have done for his parents."

"I did. I told him if he had been taken, there would have been no one to tell us that his parents needed help. I also explained that his parents would feel better knowing he was safe."

"Good. I can't help being angry at his parents for putting themselves in a position to let something like this happen." She rubbed at her temples. "Don't get me wrong, I understand the way life can weigh on you and make you feel desperate, but they have a child to think of."

"I don't know his father at all really," Deke explained, "but I feel like I know his mother pretty well. I can't see her going there. There has to be another explanation."

"Like Treat Foster," Tara suggested. "Maybe this whole thing is about him."

A thought occurred to her. She mentally toyed with it for a moment before sharing.

"What?" he asked, recognizing she'd had a revelation.

"I've been focusing on the father's coworkers at the hatchery. I think I saw him working in someone's yard last month. You know, landscaping stuff. Maybe he found the money and, considering their desperate times, kept it."

"Oh, that's brilliant."

She smiled, couldn't help herself. Deke had always had a way with compliments. "I think one of the times I saw him, Jacob was with him. Playing in the grass or something. Maybe Jacob would know the homes where he has worked."

"I'll talk to him," Deke offered. "Even if he doesn't recall the addresses, he might recognize the places if we drive him around the Hollow."

"After school tomorrow?" she asked. Every minute they waited lessened the likelihood of finding the couple alive.

"It's a date."

That was the part that worried her.

Chapter Eight

Tara logged off the computer after the department's weekly briefing. During the pandemic shutdown a few years ago, she had started attending via Zoom, as had most substations. After the shutdown was lifted, it was just easier to continue doing the same. Once a month, she attended in person.

Collin rolled his chair toward the door of Tara's office, stopping short of moving on to his own space. "So what are we supposed to do about this Agent Hanson?"

Apparently, the agent had decided to call Collin and check up on Tara's job performance. Really, why hadn't he just asked her?

Tara considered her long-time friend and work partner. "Nothing. We're supposed to be on the same side. Unless he makes an actual accusation, what can we do?"

Collin shook his head, his face arranged into an unpleasant frown. "He really made me feel uncomfortable. It was like he was looking for a way to make it appear as if you don't do your job."

That part really hadn't bothered her so much. Who knows what motive the guy had. She supposed it was possible he needed to be sure Tara was up to a missing persons case. She had been out here in the sticks, where not much had happened for a while now. Couldn't blame a guy for being concerned about a case that had been hanging over the FBI's head for three decades.

Collin shrugged. "I don't know. When he asked about your dad, that's when I really wanted to punch him. They don't come any finer than Tarrence Norwood."

"Wait." Tara quickly searched her memory of the conversation. "You didn't mention him asking about my father."

He made a face. "I didn't? I guess I was so worked up I left out that part. But he did. I was ticked off and I think he could tell."

Tara pushed up from her desk. "Exactly what did he ask about my father?"

Collin visibly concentrated on the answer before speaking. "He asked if then-Sheriff Norwood ever mentioned the Foster case. I told him I was not aware of him or you or anyone else I know mentioning Treat Foster. That happened a long time ago. Before I was born." He laughed. "He didn't appear amused by that last part."

"Sounds like a reasonable question." The words were bitter on her tongue. The idea of anyone asking a question that in any way alluded to her father's career or personal life, for that matter, being anything other than proper and aboveboard was off-putting.

Collin made a sound of distaste. "I don't like him."

Tara shrugged. "We don't have to like him, my friend, we just have to cooperate and accommodate."

Collin gave her a salute. "I'm off to follow up on that break-in over at the Duggleby cabin."

The Duggleby case was the most recent random strike by their two guys dressed in black. "Did you get a tip?"

"In a manner of speaking," he said, purposely being vague.

She lifted her eyebrows. "Your wife sensed something?"

Tara stifled a grin. Collin's wife, Patricia, once read palms for a living—still did for a few longtime clients. No offense to believers, but Tara didn't put much stock in that stuff. Although, last Christmas Patricia did say she believed the Alcott's missing dog was at the O'Linger's when no one else had—not even with missing posters up all over the Hollow— seen the animal. The Alcotts had been certain the O'Lingers had intended to keep the ridiculously expensive Lowchen. The O'Lingers, on the other hand, insisted they had rescued the dog with no collar on the side of the road miles from the Hollow.

Since the O'Lingers were elderly and spent most of their time at home, Tara figured Patricia had dropped by for an in-home reading and spotted the dog. Whatever the case, the dog was delivered to its rightful owners and the Alcotts chose not to pursue any sort of action.

"I know you don't believe her," Collin said, sounding miffed, "but some of us do."

"Hey." She held up her hands in mock surrender. "I say whatever gets the job done."

He rolled his eyes. "Anyway, she did a reading for Louise Hand and she kept seeing all kinds of colors. It was so distracting she could hardly get through the reading. When she told me the colors—orange and pink—I thought of Duggleby's cabin. Whoever broke into their cabin—"

"Took her pink-and-orange paintings," Tara finished for him. "The ones she claimed cost a mint."

"You got it. Patricia said she kept seeing hands in her vision. Louise Hand's twins have been in trouble at school over and over. Always stealing something from another kid or bullying. As a matter of fact, I talked to a couple of kids who help out with the annual fishing rodeo and they said the rumblings around school point to the Hand boys as being our guys in black."

"Sounds like a decent lead to me." She bit her lip to hold back a smile. But he was right that the Hand boys were a rowdy pair of seniors who were likely to end up in jail if they continued on their current path.

"Yeah," he growled, "I know you're a non-believer. You should try letting her do a reading for you sometime. She would change your mind. I can promise you that."

"I'll tell you what," Tara said as she reached for the keys to her Wagoneer. "Why don't you ask her what happened to Treat Foster. Or to the Callaways. I would love any kind of lead on either of those cases."

Collin sniffed. "I'll ask her."

"Thanks." She did smile then. "I appreciate it."

He called back a see-ya-later as he headed out.

Tara made it to the small lobby and the exit there when Wilma Hambrick waved from the sidewalk.

A groan rumbled in her throat, but she pasted on a smile and opened the door. "Good morning, Ms. Hambrick. How are you this morning?"

Tara knew how she was. Wilma Hambrick was unhappy. She had finished her extensive renovations on her home, burning through her husband's insurance money, and now she needed a new project. She wanted to be mayor and to be mayor she needed a city council and a police department. She needed to turn the Hollow into a city.

Tara scolded herself. In some ways, she felt a level of sympathy for the lady. Perception was very important to the older woman. The idea that the community had watched her penny-pinching life under the rule of her husband's iron fist had made her want to find some important or noteworthy way of saving face. Or proving her value and importance to the community. What better way than to become mayor?

"Oh my, I've been worried to a frazzle about that poor family that's gone missing. Is there any news?"

Tara opted not to invite the lady into her office, or she'd be in for a half hour or more briefing on the latest gossip in the Hollow.

"I'm afraid there's no news at this time," Tara said. "I was just on my way out to pick up the flyers from Ms. Tyler so I could get them posted around town."

With the internet and smartphones, most people relied on alerts from those sources. With the number of retirees in the Hollow who either had no interest in or familiarity with social media, she preferred to also add an old-fashioned method of getting the word out.

"I won't take up much of your time," Hambrick assured her.

Tara reached for patience and said what she had to say. "How can I help you?"

"You see," Hambrick began, "this is exactly why we need a full-service police department. You and Deputy Porch do all you can, but you need more. If we move forward as I'm suggesting, you'll have all the resources you need. This tragedy is a perfect example of why we need to move into the current century around here. This isn't the Hollow of forty years ago."

There was no denying life in the Hollow had changed as city dwellers moved closer in an attempt to escape the rat race of the metropolis. But really, beyond the occasional vandalism or missing dog, there was little or no crime. The recent break-ins and the missing couple notwithstanding. Wilma Hambrick had lived in the Hollow her entire life. She knew this as well as Tara did.

"I understand where you're coming from, Ms. Hambrick. I assure you we're doing all we can."

"Just remember what I said," she reiterated. "Times are changing and we need to keep up."

"You're right." Tara decided to remind the lady of the most painful part of this case. "You know, Jacob, a nine-year-old child, is the one I'm worried about. His parents are missing and they're the only family he has in the world. He's taking this very hard and he's my top priority."

Hambrick's face softened; her eyes started to shine with new emotion. "You're right, of course. It's very sad."

Tara thanked her for stopping by and followed her out of the station. She locked the door and headed for her Wagoneer. She'd spent two hours this morning reviewing any similar cases in the surrounding area. It seemed unlikely that her missing persons case was related to a serial crime spree, however, it was necessary to check.

It had occurred to her that maybe the small Dread Hollow library would have some information on Treat Foster. Though the library hadn't been open very long, Scarlett Peterson, the librarian, had lived in Dread Hollow for all her fifty-eight years. She would surely remember the Foster case. It was possible the missing Callaways had nothing to do with Foster. At this point, there was no way to conclude how they could come to be in possession of money related to that very old and very cold case.

A short drive along Main and a turn onto Sugar Alley and she was at the library. Inside, Scarlett was busy tucking away returned books. No matter how new or how small, the place had that wondrous smell of books. Tara had loved reading as a kid. Her teenage years had been filled with romance novels. She never seemed to have the time for reading these days. Or maybe it was more about the fact that she no longer put much stock in romance. Who wanted to read about happy endings if there was none to be found in her life?

Self-pity is not a good look.

"Deputy Norwood," Ms. Peterson said with a broad smile. "How nice to have you visit our little library."

"You've done a great job." Tara gave the former sweet shop a long, admiring assessment. It was the perfect replacement for the long-closed candy store. After all, the next best thing to sweets was books.

Peterson laid the book she held on the counter. "Thank you. I'm in heaven."

"I wondered if you might have a few minutes to talk about an old case."

"Oh my, that sounds so very Agatha Christie. Of course." She gestured to one of the seating areas scattered about. "We have the place to ourselves this morning. Let's relax and chat."

They settled into the comfortably upholstered chairs of the nearest seating area. "Now, tell me," Peterson said, "what case are we discussing?"

"Do you recall Treat Foster—the banker who—"

"Disappeared with half a million dollars?" she finished. "Oh yes. It was the biggest news at the time. Why, Mr. Foster was a deacon at his church. No one could believe he would just desert his wife and career that way. They had money. No one could understand why he took that money. God knows he didn't need it." She made a face. "Though, it was thought that his wife had basically cleaned him out by the time she ran off with his best friend."

Tara agreed. "It does seem strange."

"Why not just take the money from his own bank account?" Peterson shook her head. "It made no sense unless he was, indeed, broke."

"Did you know him or ever see him around the Hollow?"

Peterson relaxed into her chair, enjoying the discussion of such a juicy mystery. "I didn't know him per se, but I had met him a few times. Right here in the Hollow."

Tara's senses pricked. "Do you recall the circumstances of those meetings?"

"On the first occasion, it was early May, like now, and I was at the service station—you know, they sold gasoline back then. I had gotten out of the car to get a cola. James Ed always kept those little glass bottles on ice. It was my addiction. Mr. Foster pulled up to the pumps in his shiny automobile and requested a fill up. Before I could step out of the shop, he'd come inside and picked up a bottle of cola as well."

"Did he mention why he had come to the Hollow?" Tara had her doubts, but it didn't hurt to ask.

"No. He only smiled and mentioned what a lovely day it was."

"Was there anything else about the interaction that stayed with you?"

"I've always considered myself a fairly good judge of a person's state of mind. He seemed distracted and impatient. Perhaps not particularly happy to be here. He paid for his purchases and sped away."

"What about the other times you ran into him?" Seemed like a dead end so far.

"There were two other occasions on which I ran into him under similar circumstances. Once at the diner. I think it was summer. I recall it being quite warm. The other time, at the post office and that was between Thanksgiving and Christmas. The decorations were going up around town."

Coming here to go to the post office seemed like a bit of a drive to mail something. Unless he didn't want it postmarked in his zip code area. "Did you notice if he picked up mail or just dropped something off?"

She concentrated on the question for a moment or two. "You know, I just can't remember. I was going in. Passing through the lobby to the counter when I heard a sound and turned around. He was there. Then he left. Sorry, that's all I remember."

"You never saw him again?"

She nodded, a smile tipping up the corners of her mouth before turning to a perfect O. "Wait. Oh yes, once more. The most memorable time actually. I was visiting a friend over on Lake Trail. In one of those cute little British-style cottages."

The street where Deke lived. "Was he visiting someone there?"

"I can only assume. He was out at the lake fishing. I remember thinking how silly it was to be out there on such a miserably cold day. I believe it was in early February."

They talked a few minutes more about the strange case. When Tara felt confident she'd learned all there was to discover from the librarian, she thanked her and prepared to go.

"You know," Peterson said as she followed Tara to the door, "I wonder if they ever figured out why he took the money from only three accounts?"

Tara frowned. "Really?" She hadn't read anything about that in her research. Of course, she hadn't seen the official case file as of yet.

"I don't know if this was common knowledge," Peterson went on. "It wasn't on the news. I only heard about it because an FBI agent interviewed me. He took a call during our conversation and I heard him say to whoever had phoned him that the money was from three specific accounts, as if he'd wanted to make a statement to those account holders."

Tara would be asking Hanson about that. "Do you recall the agent's name?"

"Samuels. Roland Samuels. I'm sure he's retired or dead by now. He was fifty or so at the time."

"Thank you again, Ms. Peterson. You've been very helpful."

Tara hurried to the street and climbed into her Wagoneer. She put through a call to Hanson and got his voice mail. She left a message asking him to call her. A quick call to Regina McCall, the postmaster, who promised to look into the possibility of Treat Foster having had a post-office box. With those tasks set in motion, Tara drove to Lake Trail.

Deke's cottage was the middle one. Tara pulled into the drive of the first and got out. There was a car in the drive, so hopefully someone would be home. She knocked and waited. No sound inside. Outside was equally quiet. Any time she'd come to Deke's, she'd wondered at how very peaceful the setting was. Calm. Very calm. The view out over the water was so tranquil.

She knocked again, but there was still no sound inside. She backed out of the drive and headed to the cottage on the other side of Deke's. No vehicle in the drive. Probably no one home here either.

She hadn't quite made it to the stoop when the front door opened. "May I help you?"

The woman who spoke was seventy or so. Petite.

Soft silver hair coiled into a bun. She wore an apron and gloves as if she'd been rooting around in her garden or her flower beds.

"Hello," Tara said. "I'm Deputy Norwood and I'd like to ask you a few questions if you have a moment."

"About what?" she asked, her gaze narrowing.

"About how long you've lived on this street and who your neighbors are."

With suspicion still clouding her expression, she relented. "I've lived here for forty years. Next door, I think you know Deke. He's been here about three years."

Ah, so she'd recognized Tara. She nodded. "Yes, ma'am. Did you know the person or persons who lived there before Deke?"

"You can't be this close and not know someone, Deputy. Yes, he was a writer. He lived here for about twenty years before he moved back to France. He was French, you know."

"Before him?"

"That was Gerald Carver. A teacher at East Ridge. He was there when I moved here."

"And in the next cottage?"

"A retired stockbroker from New York," she said. "He told stories about the stock-market crash. The big one in 1929. He retired and moved here. This is where he lived until he passed away twenty-eight years ago. Now there's a former flower child who's seventy and still believes she's a twenty-year-old hippie. She's rarely home, and when she is, she doesn't answer the door. Her name is Selena Merrick. She draws. You might find her in the woods or in a field capturing the view on her sketchpad." She glanced around. "Just so you know, often I smell the odor of pot coming from her back patio. I'm certain she grows it somewhere around here."

"I'll talk to her about that," Tara offered. "One last question. Did you know Treat Foster?"

Surprise flared in the woman's expression, but she quickly concealed it. "No. I don't recognize the name. Is there some reason it should be familiar to me?"

"I was told he used to fish in this lake." Tara gestured to the water glittering beneath the sun only steps from where they stood.

"Whoever told you this was mistaken. Have a good day, Deputy."

"Wait," Tara said, barely catching her before the door closed.

At the lady's expectant expression, Tara asked, "What's your name?"

"Mia Saunders."

"Thank you. I appreciate your time."

The lady nodded and withdrew into her home, closing the door firmly behind her.

It was possible she didn't know Treat Foster, but her reaction to the question didn't quite fit that scenario.

Tara needed to talk to Deke about his neighbor.

Right now, she wished they would get a hit on the alerts that had gone out about the Callaways.

Folks around town were tying up yellow ribbons for the couple. A prayer vigil was planned for this weekend.

The couple had to be somewhere.

Chapter Nine

Tara was aware this outing could prove a dead end, but anything was better than doing nothing. Deke had spoken to Jacob and the boy confirmed his father had done a number of odd jobs besides working at the hatchery. He mowed lawns. Did a bit of carpentry work. Hauled off tree limbs and other unwanted debris as well as trash too large or too bulky for the weekly county garbage retrieval.

The Callaways had come into contact with the money somehow, and Tara needed to find that source if possible. At this time, it was the only feasible explanation for why the two were missing. Particularly since there had been no ransom demand. The large sum of money represented the single motive so far for the couple either having wronged someone or having performed a task outside the bounds of the law. People went permanently missing or toes up for far less way too often.

She hoped, for Jacob's sake, they were still alive and not guilty of an egregious crime.

Jacob strode alongside Deke. The kid's broad smile and the excitement in his step was a testament to how pleased he was to be helping with the search for his parents. Tara hoped she wouldn't have to let him down. Not all missing persons were found…and when they were, it was not always alive.

For now, she opted to continue looking on the bright side. They hadn't discovered any bodies yet.

Her determination wavered a bit when her mind wandered to more personal issues. Watching Jacob stroll toward her Wagoneer, him walking extra fast to keep up with Deke's longer strides, made her chest ache. Deke looked good with a little boy next to him. He was a great teacher and he would be an awesome father. He deserved that opportunity.

Tara would never be able to give him that.

She closed out that line of thinking. It served no purpose. What was done was done. In time, Deke would find someone new and begin the full life he deserved.

The thought made her chest ache even more fiercely.

"Fool," she muttered.

Pushing the hurt away, she propped a smile into place and said, "Hey, Jacob!"

Deke opened the back door, waited for the boy to climb inside and ensured he was secured safely in his seat.

"Hi, Deputy Tara. We're going on a field trip to find clues about my parents."

Deke laughed. "That's right, buddy. I'm certain Deputy Tara is as excited as we are."

"I am," she assured her passengers. "It's part of my job and I love my job."

Deke settled into the passenger seat next to Tara. "Since Jacob doesn't know the exact addresses," he explained, "I told him we would drive around the neighborhoods and he could watch for houses he remembers."

Deke had told her this was the case and she was good with that. Collin was back at the station following up on incoming tips. Those didn't always prove reliable, but they had to consider each one. Tara was thankful for any sort of possible lead, especially from the child of the missing couple. He might not understand that things he knew could be important. The more opportunity for comfortable exchange with him, the better the odds he would reveal some tidbit that might make a difference.

"Let's start at the beginning," Tara suggested as she pointed the Wagoneer toward the official town limits. Between that point and East Ridge, there was little in the way of anything beyond woods.

"Does that sound good to you, Jacob?" Deke asked.

The kid was already peering out the window as if he hoped to spot something right away. "Yep! I've got my Spidey binoculars." He held a pair of red-and-blue plastic binoculars sporting the Spider-Man logo. He placed them against his eyes. "I can see everything with these."

She and Deke shared a smile that had a happy warmth spreading through her chest. Tara quickly looked away, focusing on driving.

For several streets, they drove slowly up and then down while Jacob studied each house, with and without his binoculars. The silence between Tara and Deke felt heavier as the time moved at a snail's pace.

"Hey," she said, abruptly remembering his neighbors. "I checked in with your neighbors."

He glanced at her, worked up a grin. "You checking up on me?"

"No." She shook her head, shifting her gaze from his lips and how they moved so easily when he smiled, as if he did a lot of that. And he did. She knew this. His easy smile was one of the things about him that first caught her eye. "Ms. Peterson from the library mentioned having seen him fishing at the lake on Lake Trail when she was visiting a friend. Obviously, you wouldn't know since you didn't live there at the time."

"You talked to Ms. Saunders." Deke shifted a little in his seat and looked at Tara as he spoke.

She kept her gaze focused straight ahead. The less eye contact the better. "I did."

"She's a bit of a conspiracy theorist. The rumor is she has one heck of a stash of goods in her basement in the event that the balloon goes up. Don't feel bad if she was suspicious of you or your reason for knocking on her door; she's suspicious of everyone. She probably thought you were there to learn about her secret stash of guns."

Tara did look at him then. "Should I be worried about her?" Spree shootings were in the news far too often.

Deke shook his head. "I don't think so. She's just an enthusiastic prepper. She's not so tough. She calls me over to get snakes out of her yard."

Tara opted not to mention that just because the lady wouldn't shoot a snake didn't mean she wouldn't shoot a person.

"That one!"

The shout of near hysteria came from the back seat.

Tara eased to the side of the street. "Let's get out here and you show me which house you mean."

They climbed out and gathered on the sidewalk. "Point to the one you remember," Deke said.

"The yellow house over there." Jacob pointed across the street.

"Let's check it out." Tara led the way.

They congregated on the porch of the yellow house and Tara knocked on the door. She imagined that to whoever lived inside, they gave the appearance of a fundraising group or a trio inviting neighbors to church—if not for the uniform she wore.

An older gentleman opened the door. He looked

from one to the other, finally landing on Tara since she stood slightly in front of the others. "Can I help you?"

"Yes, sir." She smiled, hoping to put him at ease. Most people's concern rose when they found a deputy at their door. "I'm Deputy Norwood and we're looking for anyone who might have employed Jeff Callaway. Perhaps to cut your grass?"

He nodded, visibly relieved. His hand extended for a shake. "Richard Arrick. And yes, Jeff mowed my lawn all summer last year. He did a great job. I'm hoping he'll be able to take over for me again this year. Once the weather heats up, my heart condition puts the landscaping chores off-limits." His relief faded to concern again. "Wait, I'm not thinking. Has there been news about him and his wife?" He glanced at Jacob and managed a half-hearted smile. "Your dad is a great guy and you're a good helper. I remember you coming with him a few times."

The boy nodded. "Have you seen him? We really need to find him and my mama."

Tara's heart squeezed.

"I haven't," the man said. "But I am keeping an eye out. If I see or hear anything, I'll be sure to let you know."

"Thank you, sir." Deke took Jacob's hand. "Let's go wait in the Jeep, buddy."

Tara had agreed to allow Jacob to be involved to a degree. But when it came to the questioning, he would need to step away.

"Mr. Arrick, it sounds as if you and Mr. Callaway had a good relationship."

"We did. He's a fine young man. I was so sad to hear about his wife's cancer and then very thankful when she got better. Jeff spoke openly about how difficult that time was for them. I was happy to lend whatever support I could. My wife is a breast cancer survivor."

Cancer sucked.

Tara pushed the memories away. "Your dealings with Mr. Callaway were strictly work related?"

"Primarily, yes. He did speak often about his wife, and I offered money to help. At first, he refused to accept it unless I agreed to allow him to repay the gift with work around here. I agreed. He painted the house." He gestured to the yellow siding. "I was most pleased. I paid him five thousand dollars, which was not nearly enough in my opinion, but he would not take more."

Five thousand was a tidy sum, but it wasn't fifty. It could very well explain the twenty-five hundred. "One last question, Mr. Arrick, did you know Treat Foster?"

He made a face as if he didn't understand, then he nodded. "Oh, I see. You're referring to that bank president who stole all that money some—good gracious—twenty-five or thirty years ago."

"Yes, sir."

"I didn't. No. I read about it in the paper, of course. Why do you ask?"

"They're looking into his case again," she said, keeping the potential connection to the Callaways to herself. "Apparently, he used to spend some time in the Hollow before he disappeared. I've been asking everyone if they knew him or if they recall ever having seen him in the area."

"I don't recall ever seeing him in person." His face pinched as if he were working to dig up any potential memory. "I'm sorry I can't help you there. I will keep the Callaways in my prayers." He pointed to the yellow ribbon tied around his mailbox. "And I'm keeping that ribbon on display until they're back home."

Tara thanked him and headed to the Wagoneer. She climbed in and said to her passengers, "Off we go to the next street."

Jacob gave her a resolute nod. "I'm ready."

He seemed to enjoy being able to participate in the investigation. As unorthodox as it seemed, she firmly believed having him participate was a good idea. Not to mention they'd have to ask every resident of the Hollow without Jacob's help. This way they could pinpoint their search in the right areas.

As Tara continued her drive around the Hollow, she considered the no-answer cottage next to Deke's. "What about your other neighbor? No one answered the door when I knocked."

Deke glanced at her. "That's Selena Merrick's house. She's older, an artist, I think, and a little on the eccentric side."

Funny, Tara thought. She'd spent a good deal of

time at Deke's place when they were together and she'd never met his neighbors. Made sense now. One was a reclusive prepper, the other was an eccentric self-imposed shut-in.

"I think the one time I conversed beyond hello to Ms. Merrick, she mentioned that she bought the place about twenty years ago, so she likely wouldn't have seen Foster around. As for Ms. Saunders, I can't imagine her being friends with Foster and then pretending she hadn't known him. She would probably have seen him as some elitist who stepped on the toes of the little guy. She would have turned him in herself."

Tara laughed. "I'm sure she would have."

"Or shot him," Deke teased.

"Maybe."

She'd forgotten how much she enjoyed time with Deke. He had a way of making life feel relaxed and easy. He made even the most mundane activity feel relevant. She had missed that…missed him.

No going there. Especially with him so close.

For the next three hours, they drove the streets and roads in and around the Hollow. Collin had called to check in. He had nothing new to report. Tara had the same. Though it had not been a fruitless expedition and Jacob had certainly been gung ho. Four houses that Jacob had recognized had proven to be folks who had employed Jeff Callaway for one task or another. So far, they'd all said the same thing: super nice guy, hard worker, dependable.

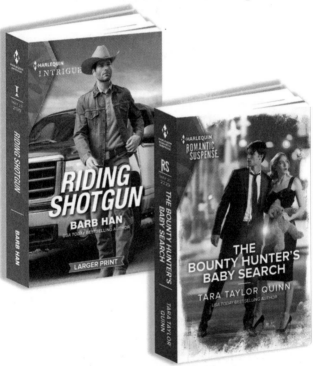

More to Love.
More to Explore.

With more to explore, we'd love to send you up to 4 BOOKS, absolutely FREE when you try the Harlequin Reader Service.

They say that "less is more" — but not when it comes to reading your favorite books!

We know that readers like you can't wait to open their newest book and settle down reading.

We feel the same way. That's why today, you can say "YES" to MORE of the great reading you love — absolutely FREE!

Try **Harlequin® Romantic Suspense** books featuring heart-racing page-turners with unexpected plot twists and irresistible chemistry that will keep you guessing to the very end.

Try **Harlequin Intrigue® Larger-Print** books featuring action-packed stories that will keep you on the edge of your seat. Solve the crime and deliver justice at all costs.

Or TRY BOTH and get 2 books from each series!

Your free books are completely free, even the shipping! If you continue with your subscription, you can look forward to curated monthly shipments of brand-new books from your selected series, always at a discount off the cover price! Plus you can cancel any time.

So don't miss out, return your Free Books Claim Card today to get your Free books.

Pam Powers

Free Books Claim Card
Say "Yes" to More Books!

YES! I love reading, please send me more books from the series I'd like to explore and a free gift from each series I select.

Get MORE to read, MORE to love, MORE to explore!

Just write in "**YES**" on the dotted line below then select your series and return this Claim Card today and we'll send your free books & gift asap!

_ _ _ YES _ _ _

Which do you prefer?

☐ **Harlequin® Romantic Suspense**
240/340 HDL GRSA

☐ **Harlequin Intrigue® Larger-Print**
199/399 HDL GRSA

☐ **BOTH**
240/340 & 199/399
HDL GRSX

FIRST NAME

LAST NAME

ADDRESS

APT.#

CITY

STATE/PROV.

ZIP/POSTAL CODE

EMAIL ☐ Please check this box if you would like to receive newsletters and promotional emails from Harlequin Enterprises ULC and its affiliates. You can unsubscribe anytime.

HI/HRS-622-LR_MMM22

How had a super nice, hard-working, reliable guy found himself in trouble?

The next road, Falling Rock Trace, Tara chose was close to the town limits going deeper into the woods and closer to the edge of the mountain. There were only three or four houses along this one.

"That one!" Jacob shouted. "That one!"

Tara slowed to a stop in the road since it was possible to see in both directions and there was zero traffic. "Which one?" She could see two up ahead, and there was the one they'd just passed.

"Behind us. The rock house."

He sounded even more excited than the previous times.

"Let's check it out." She backed up and pulled into the drive. The yard was overgrown. "You're sure about this one, Jacob?"

Whatever his father had done here, it hadn't involved landscaping. At least not lately.

"I am!" he practically shouted. "This was one of his favorites."

Tara and Deke shared an I-don't-know look and got out. Why not check it out?

The driveway was badly cracked concrete. Weeds had sprouted in the crevices. The sidewalk to the front door was the same. Cobwebs and leaves cluttered the small inset area that served as the stoop. The rounded top of the door was crusted with mud dauber nests. If anyone still lived here, they rarely used the front door.

Deke reached in front of her and swiped at the cobwebs.

"Thanks." She knocked on the door; white paint chips drifted to the stone floor.

There was no sound other than the breeze that had kicked up.

"Doesn't look like anyone lives here," Deke said.

Tara turned to their guide. "Jacob, are you sure this is one of the houses where your father worked?"

He nodded eagerly. "There's a big old apple tree around back. Come on, I'll show you."

Tara glanced around the front yard. No vehicle. "Let's check the mailbox first."

"I got it." Deke hustled back to the road and opened the door of the leaning box. He shook his head. "Empty."

"I promise this is right," Jacob urged. "Come on and I'll show you."

Tara crouched down to Jacob's eye level. "There's no one here to talk to and that's what we need. To find people who may have spoken with or seen your parents."

"Please just come around back with me."

Tara gave in. "Okay, let's have a look."

Jacob sprinted ahead as they trudged through the deep grass and weeds.

"I'm guessing this place has been empty for years," Deke said.

Tara agreed. "Keep an eye on Jacob. I want to

walk around to the other end of the house and check the electric meter."

"Hold up, buddy," Deke called after Jacob.

Tara picked her way along the back side of the house. There were curtains drawn tight over all the windows. More cobwebs and mud dauber nests. She rounded the far corner and confirmed her conclusion. There was no meter. It had been pulled. No meter, no electricity. No electricity, no lights or heat.

She moved on to the front of the house and gauged the distance to the next two houses on the road. More than half a mile, for sure. If there was anyone home at either of those houses, they could maybe confirm when this house had last been occupied. With that in mind, Tara walked around to the back side of the house again.

Jacob had been right. A large apple tree stood in the center of the yard. He and Deke were walking around the yard where it disappeared into the tree line. The woods along this road were thick and old. Knowing the local terrain, she estimated it wasn't far to the bluff once you entered those woods.

Dusk was creeping in. They should load up, and she would stop by the other two houses before heading back to the Wright home to drop off Jacob. Or maybe she would take both Jacob and Deke back to his vehicle at the school. The latter would prevent her from spending alone time with Deke.

She really should suck it up and be an adult about

this thing. They were over and there was no need to constantly be on guard. Just move on and treat Deke like any other citizen of the Hollow. Wouldn't that be nice? If only she could pretend away the feelings that wouldn't let go. The dreams that haunted her sleep. All the little things that reminded her of him and their time together.

The need that tore at her like a beast any time she saw him.

Too bad it seemed like that feat was impossible.

How long would it take, she wondered, to reach that place where she no longer felt such an intense desire…the longing to be with him?

Collin was right, she supposed. She needed to start dating again and that would make the transition easier. Except, she hadn't been able to make herself manage so much as a meal with anyone else.

She was hopeless.

"Jacob, wait!"

Tara's senses alerted. She turned back to see where Jacob and Deke were. Jacob was nowhere to be seen and Deke was rushing into the tree line.

"Jacob!" Tara shouted as she rushed in that direction. It took a hell of a push, but she managed to catch up with Deke. "Where is he?" she demanded without slowing down.

Deke dodged a group of trees. She did the same.

"He just took off." He glanced at Tara. "We have to catch him before it gets dark."

He didn't have to say the rest: *the cliffs*.

Tara pushed even harder, zigzagged through the trees.

Where the hell was the kid going?

Chapter Ten

Jacob ran as fast as he could.

Even though it had been a while since he was here, he remembered the way.

Mr. D and Deputy Tara were calling for him. He felt bad for running like this, but he'd made a promise to his dad.

His dad had showed him this place but made him promise never to tell anyone about it.

Jacob ran harder. He couldn't let them catch up with him. They would make him go back to Ms. Wright's house. He liked Ms. Wright, but he wanted to be with his mama and dad.

They could be waiting for him. He hadn't thought of that until today when Mr. D mentioned driving around to look for the places his dad did work. Jacob realized then that maybe his mama and dad were here waiting for him to come so they could all be together again. Maybe they had escaped the bad men and hidden.

Limbs from the bushes slapped him in the face

and dragged at his legs, but he had to keep going. Almost there.

The ground disappeared from under his feet, and he pitched forward.

Jacob bit down hard to stop from crying out, pinching his tongue. The sting brought tears to his eyes. He hit the leaf-covered ground and rolled a good way before he could stop himself.

He jumped up. Steadied himself. The woods spun round and round. His heart beat against his chest so hard he was sure it would pop out any second like that alien in that movie he watched one night when his parents were working late.

He sucked in more air. Tried to figure out where he was.

Then he saw it. The old dead tree that stood near the cave opening—the mouth, his dad had called it.

He started that way. He heard his friends calling for him. They were going the wrong way.

He felt bad. They were his friends. They were taking care of him and trying to help him.

Jacob stared up at the sky. It was almost dark. He had to hurry.

He picked his way through the bushes and between the trees until he reached the dead one. A big, tall oak that, his dad said, had probably been struck by lightning a long time ago. He said it was probably just a shell now, waiting for the right gust of wind to take it down.

Jacob's heart started pumping hard again as he

peered into the cave. The opening was as tall as him and a lot wider. For a grown-up it didn't look that big, but to him it was good sized. It was pretty dark in there and he didn't have a flashlight.

Didn't matter. All he had to do was call out to them, and if they were here, they would come get him. He eased deeper into the cave and called out as loudly as he dared, "Mama! Dad! Are you here?"

There was a sound…dripping. Water dripping. His dad said that was normal in caves. It was a lot cooler in here. He moved slowly, remembering the uneven rocks on the floor. They could be slick.

"Mama! Dad! Are you here?"

Something heavy felt as if it pushed against his chest, but there was nothing there. It was inside. It got heavier and heavier until he could hardly breathe. His eyes burned with the pain of understanding.

They weren't here.

His mama and dad might never come back and he would be all alone forever.

Chapter Eleven

"Do you see him?" Tara pushed through the brush. Her face stung from the limbs slapping at her. Her lungs burned from the hard run.

"I don't see him," Deke said from a dozen yards away. "Jacob!"

How could a nine-year-old boy move that fast?

Tara stalled. Took a couple of gulps of air. She and Deke were no threat to Jacob. He wasn't afraid of them. The only way he would feel this confident running headlong into the woods with it nearly dark was if he knew where he was going.

"Deke!" She headed in his direction. His voice echoed as he called again for Jacob.

Tara caught up with him. He shook his head, took a gasp of air. "Why the hell would he run from us?"

"He's not." Tara pushed the strands of hair that had been pulled free of her ponytail away from her face. "He's running toward something. There has to be an old shack or campsite. Something. He's been there before and feels like he needs to go back."

Deke's gaze collided with hers. "Caves. There are caves in these woods."

He was right. "You keep looking," she suggested. "I'm calling for backup. We can't risk him getting lost out here. There's wildlife in these woods too."

"Mr. D!"

Relief shot through Tara's veins.

Deke took off in the direction of the boy's voice. Tara followed. Thank God. Thank God.

A crashing sound drew them to the left and suddenly Jacob emerged from a line of trees surrounded by shoulder-high shrubs and brush.

He ran to Deke. Slammed into him almost knocking him off his feet. Sobs rocked his slim body.

Deke dropped to his knees and hugged the weeping child. "What happened, buddy?"

Tara moved and crouched down to see his face better. "You okay?"

"I'm sorry I ran from you." He swiped at his eyes with his fists. "I had to go to the cave and see if they were there waiting for me."

"Your parents?" Tara's tension moved to a higher level. "Were you parents supposed to be waiting here for you?"

He shrugged, his face crumpled in a mixture of fear and grief. "I don't know. My dad brought me here a couple of times. He said the cave was a special place. A good hiding place. He said if we ever needed a place to hide until it was safe, this would be the place." He swiped hard at his eyes again, frustrated with the tears and obviously unable to slow them. "I thought they might have gotten away from the bad guys and come here to hide and wait for me."

"Did your dad tell you they would come here and wait for you?"

Jacob stared at the ground. Shook his head. "No. I was just hoping, I guess."

"I'm sorry, buddy," Deke said softly.

"Jacob," Tara said, drawing his gaze to her, "can you show us where the cave is. I have my flashlight. I should probably have a look around."

He nodded and motioned for her to follow him. She and Deke shared another of those worried glances. This kid had been through hell without once showing it, but staying strong was getting to him. Today he'd reached his breaking point. Poor kid.

When they arrived at the mouth of the cave, Tara was surprised at how well concealed it was. The opening was not very large. She took her flashlight from her utility belt and turned to Deke. "Keep him close to you. I'll have a look inside."

"No way. Give me the flashlight. I've been in more caves than you have."

"Deke," she warned.

"No offense, Deputy," he said, holding out his hand, "the facts are the facts. Part of being brave is being smart."

Reluctantly, she handed him the flashlight. Then she reached for Jacob's hand. "We will figure this out, Jacob."

He nodded, but he didn't look at her. It didn't take much imagination to understand that he was losing faith. He was scared and needed his parents.

What the hell had they done?

Fifteen minutes later, Deke exited the cave.

"I was just about to come in after you," she said, thankful to see his face again. Damn it.

"It's not such a wide cave," he told her, "but it's deep. It goes on and on, and there are corridors that go off in different directions. We'll need to be a good deal more prepared if we're going exploring in there. I've been lost once or twice and it's not a good feeling."

"We'll come back tomorrow," she suggested. "Let's get this guy home. I'm sure he's exhausted."

Deke handed her flashlight back to her and took Jacob's hand in his. "Let's go find some pizza and ice cream. I'm starving."

Jacob smiled. "Chocolate ice cream with sprinkles?"

"You got it," Deke promised.

The walk back to the house was longer and more exhausting than the rush into the woods, mostly because it was uphill and adrenaline had robbed her of strength. The good news was Jacob was okay. They hadn't lost him and they'd learned something more about his father. He thought about contingency plans. There had to be a reason. Some people worried about their children's futures and bought life insurance and stocks. Other people worried about the government taking over their lives and prepped for bugging out, like Deke's neighbor. Whatever the case, there was always, always a reason.

When they reached the backyard, Tara studied the dark house lit only by the moon that was out now. How long had the house been abandoned? Who had lived here?

"Jacob, did your dad know the person who lived here?"

"Maybe. He used to bring his riding lawn mower here and cut the grass. He came a bunch of times last year. But he only came once this year. That's when he showed me the cave."

But the grass hadn't been cut. "Did he bring his lawn mower when the two of you came this year?"

"No. We just came in his truck." He shrugged. "I mean we had the trailer and lawn mower, but he didn't use it."

"Did the two of you ever go inside the house?"

Jacob moved his head side to side in a firm no. "We cut the grass or visited the cave."

"Thanks, Jacob, for helping us today," Tara said. "You're really smart. Your mom and dad will be proud when they find out how much you've helped us."

They started toward the front of the house. Tara was ready for a long hot shower. She was sure poor Jacob was ready to crash. Probably the only thing keeping him upright was the promise of pizza and chocolate ice cream with sprinkles.

As they reached the Wagoneer, a vehicle coming from the direction of the other houses farther up the road slowed to a stop. The driver powered his window down.

"Deputy Norwood?"

Tara left Deke and Jacob to climb into the Wagoneer and approached the vehicle stopped on the road.

"Evening, sir," she offered.

He gave a nod of acknowledgment. "Brandon Parton. I live in the first house on the right back that way." He jerked his head in the direction from which he'd come. "Did my wife finally call about the lights we saw a few nights ago? That house has been empty for years, and last week, maybe on a Wednesday, as I was driving by, I saw a flashlight bobbing around in there. I almost stopped to check it out, but I had my granddaughter with me. Then I just plain forgot."

"No one called. I'm glad you didn't stop and go in. It's never safe to approach the scene of a potential crime. Better to call it in."

"Yeah, that's what my wife said too. I didn't really figure she'd called, but she saw the lights that night and said she'd seen them once or twice before and figured it was just some homeless person seeking refuge from that last frosty night. My wife is a bit of a softie. Like me, she knows the place was basically abandoned. Someone might as well take shelter there."

Tara smiled her understanding. "Do you know who owns the house?"

He frowned. "I'm embarrassed to say I don't.

When we moved here about fifteen years ago, I was told a woman lived there. Later I heard she'd moved away. I'm not sure anyone really knows."

"The other house down the road, who lives there?"

"Ed Kosh. He lived there for forty years. He passed about six months ago. His house is being renovated for listing on the market."

"Thank you, Mr. Parton. We'll investigate the lights and make sure no one is vandalizing the place."

"Thank you," he said, then he backed up in the road and turned around to go back home.

Tara walked back to her Wagoneer. She opened the door and ducked inside. "That was Mr. Parton, who lives in the next house down the road. He has seen someone with a flashlight in the house, so I'm going to have a quick look before we go."

Jacob had drifted off to sleep in the back seat. Deke glanced at the boy and then looked to her. "I would argue with you going in alone, but I know it would be pointless, so I'll stay here with Jacob and you do what you have to do."

"Thanks."

That was one of the hardest parts of being a woman and a cop. Most men were protective by nature. Having a woman do the protecting was kind of an ego punch. She had to admit, Deke had handled it well when they were a couple.

Tara used her flashlight to guide her since it was fully dark now. She pulled on a pair of gloves and checked the front door. It was locked. Checked the windows since there were several across the front. All the ones in front were either locked or painted shut. She made her way around the south end. Windows were locked. She found the same along the back wall. When she reached the small patio and the back door, she was startled to find that door unlocked. Not damaged or tampered with, just unlocked.

She stepped inside, leaving the door open behind her. "Sheriff's Department," she called out, "is anyone inside the house?"

Her voice echoed through the silence. She roved her flashlight methodically over the space. Kitchen. Very late-seventies decor with harvest-gold appliances and faux-looking wood cabinets.

She made a face. The house smelled like dead flowers. But then she had no idea how long it had been closed up. A few steps across the fake-brick linoleum, and she opened the fridge. There were items inside, but the decomp process had long ago completed and formed hard globs of whatever. Cheese, maybe? She shuddered. A carton of milk that had expired in 1999 sat in the middle of the largest shelf.

The kitchen cabinets were the same, mostly empty. The few canned and dry goods had expired decades ago. An old rotary phone hung on the wall. The curly cord hung to the floor. The kitchen and dining room were one rectangular room. A table and chairs with matching china cabinet, china still inside, filled that end of the room.

The living room was pretty much the same. Vintage furniture. Layers of dust. Old newspapers and magazines on the coffee table. Gold-and-brown shag carpet on the floor. Didn't smell any better in the living room or in the hall as she made her way to the bedrooms. She had decided the smell was sort of like that cave. Musty and dank. She doubted any sunlight made it past the heavy curtains on all the windows.

The first two bedrooms were open. Had the same shag carpet and were furnished in a style consistent with the rest of the house. The bathroom was dusty with those gold-flecked four-inch square tiles covering the walls about halfway up. The gold fixtures were discolored with age.

The final bedroom door was closed. Tara opened the door and instantly understood where the foul odor was coming from. The scene was far different from the rest of the house.

Newspapers stood in waist-high stacks around the perimeter of the room. She shifted the beam of light to the bed. There was a lump under the covers. She followed the form until the glow of her flashlight lit on two dark holes in a skull.

She almost stumbled back. Caught herself and steadied the beam of light. "Damn."

The owner hadn't moved; she or he had died in bed.

Tara moved closer. Tried to determine if the remains belonged to a man or a woman. The hair was longish. Whatever clothing he or she had worn was too far gone to categorize. The color might have been a green, but it was difficult to make a true assessment.

The petrified remains were tucked under the covers. The smell wasn't good but not as bad as she would have expected. She moved closer, almost tripped over the remains of what she presumed to be a dog on the floor. It appeared to have passed while curled up in its bed asleep. She leaned down and spotted the collar. Dog for sure, she decided. *Butch* was engraved on the tag.

Tara shook herself and focused on continuing to review the scene. So far, she saw nothing that marked it as a crime scene, just a sad ending to two lives.

She walked to where the newspapers stood in neat rows. Local papers—back when they were still in circulation.

The headlines on one were circled. *Foster Still Missing.*

No big surprise. The case was big news thirty years ago and for a good number after that. There had been a true-crime show or two about it.

She walked around to the other side of the bed where a small table topped with a lamp stood. She opened the one drawer and surveyed the contents. Handkerchief. Eye glasses. Prescription bottles. She checked the labels. The dates showed the medications had been filled in January thirty years ago. Tara recognized one as being for pain. She did an internet search on the other. Also for pain. Oddly there was no name of the patient or the physician on the bottles. She placed the bottles back in the drawer. Noted a photo lying loose. The photograph was old. Black-and-white. A young girl and boy stood together holding hands. Judging by their clothes, this was something from fifty or more years ago. She turned over the photo to look for anything that might be written on the back. Many of the photographs from her childhood were labeled that way.

Treat and me. The date was listed, but it was the name *Treat* that had Tara startled. The boy might have been twelve or thirteen, the girl maybe ten. She glanced back at the bed, the beam of her flashlight falling on the skull with its leathery skin remains and thin clumps of hair. Was this Treat Foster's sister or friend? Was she, presumably, the reason he'd come here repeatedly before his disappearing act?

Tara set the photo back in the drawer and called Collin. She gave him the address and asked him to come right away. She wasn't leaving this scene unattended now that she'd discovered it. Then she called Sergeant Snelling. He wasn't going to believe this. She didn't believe it, but she was here, looking at it.

A little voice suggested she call Agent Hanson, but she shut out that voice. She would call him when she had a better handle on what they had. No need to drag him all the way out here and get his hopes up for nothing. The person who had lived in the house may have found these items and kept them.

This was not likely, but Tara was going with it for now.

She walked out the front door, peeled off the gloves and found Deke pacing next to the Wagoneer.

He stopped when he saw her. "You find anything?"

She waited until she was next to him to explain. Voices carried in the dark and she could almost see the neighbor with his head hanging out a window to hear what was going on.

"Jacob still out?" she asked.

"Yeah. Poor kid was exhausted after getting his hopes up like that only to have them dashed."

"There are human remains inside," she told Deke. "So I can't leave until Collin gets here. He should arrive any minute. Sorry to keep you hanging around like this. If you want to take Jacob to the Wrights and then go home, Collin can give me a ride later."

"No thanks. I'm staying with you."

She had known that would be his answer.

"You think the owner just died in there and no one ever noticed?" he asked.

It happened. "Possibly. Some folks don't have any family, and if they don't have friends or people they socialize with, there's no one to check on them." Damned depressing way to go.

"That's sad," he said, his gaze fixed on the house. "No one should die alone."

Unless she went first, Tara would have no family left when her dad passed away. She did have her work, but she could be retired by then. She didn't belong to any social groups or a church. Would she end up that way?

How pathetic was it that she didn't even have a dog to see her out?

"There was a dog," she told him. "Butch. He stayed with her or him."

Deke heaved a heavy breath. "I don't want to go like that. Alone, I mean."

"Who does?" she pointed out, avoiding making her response personal.

He moved closer to her and leaned against the side of the Wagoneer. "Whatever happens in the future, I'll keep tabs on you, Tara. I'll call. Drop by. Whether you want me to or not."

She ignored the warm sensation that accompanied his words. "That might be considered stalking."

"Then Collin can arrest me, but that's what I'm going to do."

No matter that she had pretended dying alone didn't bother her, he understood it did, and he said those words to ensure she knew he would be around, like it or not. That was the kind of guy he was. Caring. Kind.

What was wrong with her?

How had she walked away from this man?

As if she'd stated the words aloud, he said, "I learned my lesson over the past six months. I'm not going to pretend I don't care about you. You're stuck with that, you got it?"

She nodded as she leaned against cool metal next to him. "Got it."

They could be friends.

His arm went around her shoulders and pulled her

close. He whispered, his lips so close to her forehead she could feel them move, "I will change your mind if it takes me the rest of my life."

She wanted desperately to turn her face up to his and feel his lips against hers.

Collin pulled up and saved Tara from herself.

Or maybe she couldn't be saved.

The jury was still out on that score.

Chapter Twelve

Collin stalled in the doorway of the last bedroom in the house. "Man, oh man. How long you think she's been here?"

Tara considered the room in the better lighting. Collin had brought the portable lighting and generator from his garage. The skeletal remains looked even more eerie in the brighter light.

"About thirty years if the information on those prescription bottles is accurate." Tara had seen a few bodies in her early cop days but never one this far along in the decomposition process. "The clothing and bed linens are still intact for the most part. I'm sure Snelling will be able to tell us more." She checked the time on her cell. "He and his team should be here soon."

"Should we do some more looking around?"

He knew the answer. "We should wait for Snelling. I've already had a closer look than I should have."

"You think she died of natural causes?"

"I'm guessing so. The prescriptions were for pain meds."

"Hell of a way to go." Collin grimaced. "All alone like this." He shrugged. "Except for the dog. At least she had a companion."

Tara hadn't been able to stop thinking about dying alone since she walked into this room. The thought had her reliving the things Deke had said to her... the way his lips had brushed her temple.

She exiled the thoughts. What was wrong with her? She was standing in the middle of a room with a thirty-year-old corpse and she couldn't keep Deke out of her head. Not good. Maybe she'd had this cushy nothing-ever-happens-in-Dread-Hollow job too long. She'd lost her edge.

As soon as Collin had arrived, she'd had him drive Deke and Jacob back to the school to get his truck. She hadn't been able to think as clearly with Deke here...so close.

She set her mind back to the here and now. No more reminiscing. "We should head back out to meet Snelling."

"The neighbor didn't have a clue?" he asked on the way to the front door.

"He thought the place was empty." Tara considered the nearly knee-deep grass around the house. Why wasn't it deeper? Why weren't the shrubs and hedges up to the roof? At home, the crepe myrtles would take over if they weren't trimmed annually.

The boxwoods required far more attention. Jacob said his father had cut the grass here last year. Maybe he'd trimmed all the shrubs too. But they hadn't done any trimming this year. Considering the corpse— presumably the owner—couldn't have hired him, then who?

"The team's here," Collin said from the door.

Tara followed him out to greet Snelling and his team. Tara brought him up to speed on what she'd found inside. She didn't mention the photo for now. Snelling would want to call Hanson before proceeding. Tara's gut said she should hang on to the scene for a bit longer. Jacob had said his father worked at this house, which meant maybe there was a connection between the missing couple and Treat Foster, slim though it might be, or the person who had died in the house.

In Tara's opinion, her missing persons case took priority over a thirty-year-old cold case.

While Snelling's crew carried in more lights and the other equipment they would need, Tara signaled for Collin to join her away from the others. "I need to check out a couple of things. Can you stay here until I get back?"

"Sure thing. Let me know if you need me."

Tara backed out of the drive and headed toward the neighbor's house. She pulled into the neighbor's drive and exited the Wagoneer. Mr. Parton was obviously watching the activity next door since the porch light came on and he was at the front door before she reached it.

"Looks like you've found something amiss over there," he said.

"I'm afraid I can't give you specifics, but the answer is yes. You mentioned the house appeared to be empty since you moved here."

"That's right. Ed, the neighbor who passed recently, said he'd never seen anyone there either. He lived here for nearly twenty-five years."

"Someone was cutting the grass or it would be considerably more overgrown," she said in hopes of prompting information on who had hired Jacob's father.

"Oh, yes, you're right. Ed paid someone to come about once a month to cut the grass and prevent the shrubs from getting out of hand. He thought it devalued his property when a neighboring house was all grown up." He gave a nod. "I suppose it'll be up to me now."

"Mr. Kosh never mentioned who he hired?"

Parton shook his head. "Recently, I noticed a small red truck. An older truck. There was a lawn mower on one of those small black metal trailers behind it. The vehicle was parked on the side of the road in front of the house. I never saw anyone in the yard though. Since Ed passed, I suppose I should have stopped to speak with whoever was driving the truck."

Jeff Callaway drove a small red truck.

"Thank you, Mr. Parton. You've been a great help." She gave him one of her cards. "Please call me if you remember anything else or see anyone not in an official vehicle hanging around the house." She smiled. "My Wagoneer is my official vehicle."

"I'll remember that."

Tara thanked him again and hurried back to her vehicle. She made her way back to what she decided to call the bone house. "Morbid, Tara," she muttered as she parked behind Collin's cruiser.

Bright light simmered behind the curtains, creating a kind of eerie glow outside each window. She pulled on shoe covers and gloves and stepped inside. Between Collin's lights and the ones Snelling's team had brought, the place was lit up like an airport terminal.

Collin was in the kitchen. Tara joined him there. "Anything new?"

"Not that I've been told about." He hitched his head toward the other end of the house. "You know Snelling, he's pretty tight-lipped until he has a good handle on things."

"He'll fill us in when he can. I spoke to the nearest neighbor, Mr. Parton. The other neighbor, a Mr. Kosh, who died recently, had been paying someone to cut the grass and clip the shrubs about once a month during the summer. He felt the overgrown property adversely impacted the value of his."

"I can see how he'd feel that way," Collin agreed. "No one likes a dump next door."

"Mr. Parton says the vehicle he saw at this property most recently was a small red truck with a trailer and lawn mower. That confirms what Jacob told me."

"That gives us a concrete connection between the two cases," Collin pointed out.

"I'm guessing this is where the money came from."

"Based on the photo you found in the bedroom," Collin offered.

"Exactly. If the person who lived here was somehow connected to Foster, this may have been his hiding place."

Collin surveyed the kitchen. "So there could be half a million dollars hidden around here somewhere."

"Maybe. The real question in my mind," Tara said, "is whether whatever Callaway came upon here is the reason he and his wife are missing?"

"We need to know more about the person who lived in this house," Collin offered.

"I'll call Helen over at property records." She checked the time on her cell. "It's late, but maybe she can find the owner's name for us. Then I'm going to see Delilah. She and her family know everyone in this town. I need you to stay here for a while and keep me up to speed on what's happening."

He nodded. "Will do."

Tara had just reached the front door when Agent Hanson opened it.

He glared at her. "You weren't going to call me about this find."

It wasn't a question. It was a flat-out accusation. Snelling had obviously called him.

"I had no reason to believe I should call you, Agent Hanson." This was a lie, but sometimes a little white lie was necessary.

"Sergeant Snelling has found a number of items that connect this scene to the Foster case."

"I also found a connection to the Callaway case."

"I'm not going to war with you over who has jurisdiction. I'm investigating a federal case that involves possibly one or more homicides."

"What you have," Tara argued, "is a thirty-year-old cold case about missing money and remains from a probable death by natural causes. I, on the other hand, have two missing persons right now. I don't think you'll win this war."

"Until I hear otherwise," Hanson warned, "I'm not backing off."

"Suit yourself." Tara turned her back on him and went back to the kitchen. She pulled Collin aside. "The one thing about the Foster case we've learned is that he took money from only three accounts. Do you still have that cousin in the Chattanooga Police Department?"

"Sure do."

"See if she has a contact with the Bureau who can give her the names of those three victims. She may have copies of relevant FBI statements and reports in their case file. Whatever she can find would be immensely useful. If there's a Dread Hollow resident among those three, we need to know."

"On it. I'll go outside and call. She's a night owl like me. She won't mind a call after business hours."

"Thanks, Collin. Let me know what you find out. I'm going to Delilah's house."

Hanson had already disappeared into the bedroom end of the house. Just as well, Tara had nothing else to say to him.

Outside, the breeze had picked up, giving Tara a chill. She settled behind the wheel of her Wagoneer, sent a text to Delilah and headed into town. It was nearly ten and Main Street was rolled up for the night. Delilah lived just a mile down Dread Hollow Road beyond Tara's house. Thankfully, the lights were still on. Tara hadn't received a response to her text and she'd worried her friend had crashed for the night.

Exhaustion had started to claw at Tara by the time she made her way to Delilah's porch. Her cell chirped. Delilah. The message said she should come on in. Tara opened the door and stepped inside the old farmhouse. The house was warm and smelled of something sweet. Delilah's house always smelled like something freshly baked.

"I'm here," Tara called out.

"In my office," Delilah shouted back.

Delilah's house had the same wood floors as hers. Tara was fairly certain her great-great-grandfather and Delilah's grandfather had worked together to build the houses. Neighbors helped each other build back in those days.

The family room was large with the same vaulted ceiling and massive fireplace. Delilah had turned the small downstairs bedroom into an office. Tara was thinking of doing the same; she just hadn't gotten around to it yet.

Delilah was hunched over her desk tallying up the day's receipts. She liked doing things the old-fashioned way. Everything she served in the diner was made from scratch.

"Any news on Krissy and her husband?" Delilah pulled off her glasses and gestured to the chair that sat at one end of her desk.

"We've picked up some additional information here and there, but no hint of who may have taken them." Tara collapsed into the chair, suddenly realizing how very tired she was. "It's the strangest case. We can assume the motive is money, but that doesn't make sense either considering we found a sizeable sum in their home. If the perps were going to take the couple, why not the cash?"

Delilah rubbed the bridge of her nose with her thumb and forefinger. "It just makes no sense. Krissy and her husband would never hurt anyone. They've never been in trouble as far as I know."

Tara shook her head. "I ran checks on both of them. Nothing." She braced her elbow on Delilah's desk and rested her chin in her hand. "We drove Jacob around the Hollow so he could point out places he recalled his father having done odd jobs."

"We? You and Collin?" Her eyes sparkled teasingly. She knew the answer. Word traveled fast around the Hollow.

"Deke and I."

"Are you two talking again?" She held up both hands, fingers crossed.

"Jacob is his student. We're working together for him."

Delilah dropped her hands. "Oh. I see."

Did everyone—including Tara's father—believe she and Deke belonged together?

"It's best if he moves on. I'm not what he needs," Tara reminded her friend.

Delilah's expression turned knowing.

"No," Tara said before she could ask, "I didn't tell him."

Delilah's expression shifted to surprise. "Why?"

"Because he would have said it didn't matter." Was she the only one who recognized what Deke wanted in his future? "He loves kids. Have you not noticed? It would have mattered, but he would have pretended it didn't just to keep me happy. I know him, Dee."

"I feel like I know him fairly well myself and I think you're wrong," her friend argued.

"That's the sort of man he is," Tara maintained. "Honorable. Kind to a fault. He would have insisted it didn't matter and we would have taken that big plunge into wedded bliss that would have lasted a little while. Then he would have grown bitter and started to resent me."

"I think you're underestimating the man."

"Please," Tara countered. "I'm not. I'm simply choosing not to allow him to sacrifice what he wants to fit in with what I can't have."

"People adopt children. Children who need families to love them."

"Moving on," Tara said, unable to talk about it any longer. "There are three houses on Falling Rock Trace, are you familiar with the people who own them?"

Delilah thought about the question for a moment. "Everyone knows Brandon Parton and his wife, Carla. There's Ed Kosh, who died a few months back. His wife died years ago. The other homeowner is barely known at all. Melanie Grant, if I'm recalling correctly. She moved to the Hollow years and years ago. When I was about your age." Delilah laughed. "Mercy, how time flies. Anyway, she kept to herself. Never spoke to anyone on the rare occasions when she ventured into town. She had most things delivered. Pete Bishop, who used to run the market, would make deliveries. He had a reputation as a lady's man, so of course there were rumors. She didn't go to church, which alone, as you well know, made her an outsider. I suppose she eventually moved away. I just remember not seeing her or hearing about her anymore."

A sad story for sure. Deke's words whispered through her again.

"Why do you ask?" Delilah prompted.

"Jeff did some work at the house. Kosh hired him to keep the grass and shrubs trimmed. Jacob seemed to know the place well."

"Ed would do that," Delilah agreed. "I've driven by a couple of times over the years and it always looked deserted to me."

Tara nodded. "We found human remains in one of the bedrooms. I don't know if it's her, but someone died in the home. Nothing is confirmed yet, so what I've just told you is for your ears only."

"Sure. Sure." She frowned. "That's so sad."

"Were there ever any rumors about her and Treat Foster?"

Surprise again flashed across Delilah's face. "Nothing comes immediately to mind, but the time frame of when she was still about works. Do you think there was an affair going on? Maybe that's why he was suspected of coming to the Hollow from time to time."

"I have no idea, but it would be helpful to find out all we can."

"I'll make some quiet inquiries of those old enough to remember the Hollow's recluse. That's what the kinder folks called her. A recluse."

"Any information you can dig up would be helpful."

Delilah studied her face a moment. "I'm going to have to ply you with coffee or send you home. You look ready to fall out."

Tara pushed to her feet. "I'm off. Thanks for making time for me at this hour."

"You are welcome any time." Delilah showed her to the back door, but hesitated. "Wait, I baked cookies." She walked to the island in the center of the big kitchen and grabbed a tin—the kind Christmas cookies came in. She handed it to Tara. "It's a new recipe. Take it to the office tomorrow and let me know if you like it."

Tara smiled. "Collin will be over the moon."

"I'll call you with anything I learn," Delilah promised.

Tara waved good-night and plodded out to the Wagoneer. The drive home took all of a minute, maybe a minute and a half. The house was dark. Once again, she'd forgotten to leave on a light. But then it wasn't often that she was out this late.

She climbed out of the vehicle and slogged to the side porch. A quick twist of her key and she was in. She debated waiting until morning to shower but felt as if decades of dust and decomposition were layered on her skin.

Rather than pop into the kitchen for a nightcap or food, she left the cookies on the nearest table and went straight upstairs, peeling off her clothes on the way. She'd made it to the bathroom, dropped her uniform on the floor and turned on the shower when her cell rang.

Deke.

"Hey, everything okay?" Her heart instantly beat

faster. She told herself it was because he could be calling to report trouble with Jacob, but really it was only because he was calling.

"I hadn't heard from you. You make it home okay?"

"Just now," she said, holding her phone between her cheek and shoulder so she could unfasten her bra. The garment fell away and she sighed with relief.

"You sound tired."

He had no idea. The panties went next. "I was just getting in the shower."

Silence echoed on the other end.

Frowning, she reached for a towel and slung it over the shower curtain rod. "You still there?"

"Sorry the image of you naked and getting in the shower just exploded in my brain."

She wanted to say something emphasizing her shock, but she was too busy navigating the intense heat rushing through her.

"Who said I was naked?"

He laughed, the sound deep and a little rough. "I don't remember you getting in the shower with your clothes on."

She stared at her reflection in the full-length mirror that hung on the wall next to the vintage sink. Her breasts tingled and she suddenly felt damp in places she had no right to as exhausted as she was.

"I remember every inch of your body. Smooth, soft skin. Firm, rounded bottom. And God, your breasts. Sorry. I...I should let you get in the shower."

For a moment, she couldn't speak, her throat had constricted with yearning.

She wanted to tell him she remembered every inch of him as well. Broad shoulders. Narrow waist with those perfect abs. Long, thick legs.

She had to hang up.

"Bye," she muttered and ended the call.

She braced against the sink and wondered how the hell she could be perched on the brink of an orgasm just hearing his voice.

She ducked into the shower and savored the steaming water while her body betrayed her and her mind refused to exile images of the man she'd loved with all her heart.

Still loved.

She forced the thought away, cried out with anger and physical release at the same time.

Then she slid down the wall of the shower and hugged herself while she cried for everything that would never be.

Chapter Thirteen

A sound woke Jacob.

He listened. It was dark. Not time to get up yet. The house was quiet. Everyone was asleep.

Why'd he wake up?

He reached down to the floor where Jelly Bug lay sleeping. She didn't even lift her head when Jacob rubbed it. She was out too.

Jacob closed his eyes and tried to go back to sleep.

He heard the sound again.

A pecking at the window. He rolled to the other side of the bed and got up. He walked to the window. The sound came again. *Peck. Peck. Peck.*

What if it was his dad? He might have come to get him.

Jacob moved the curtain aside. Someone was outside the window, but it was too dark to see who it was. A hand wearing a glove waved at him.

Jacob pressed his face closer to the window. "Who are you?"

"Your daddy sent me," the voice whispered. "He

said to bring you and Jelly Bug to him. Your mom is there too."

"How do I know you're telling the truth?" Jacob was no dummy. He knew all about stranger danger.

One hand used a cell phone to shine light on something dangling from the other hand. A cross necklace.

His dad's necklace. Jacob's heart beat harder. This person really had been sent by his dad. He unlocked the window and pushed it up just a crack.

He felt scared again. What if this was a trick? "You got any other proof?"

The hand showed him a ring. "Your mom sent this."

It was his grandmother's ring. His mom never took it off. But this was an emergency. She knew Jacob would never believe a stranger without proof.

"What do I have to do?" Jacob asked.

"Hand me the dog first."

Jacob hurried around the bed and picked up Jelly Bug. She felt heavy and limp in his arms. What was wrong with this dog? Her head just hung down, but she was still breathing. Jacob moved back to the window, but it wasn't open wide enough. The hand reached in and pushed it upward. Jacob hefted the dog out the window.

"Now you climb out. Your parents are waiting."

Jacob climbed out the window, then closed it.

His mama and dad hadn't left him.

He took the stranger's gloved hand and walked into the night.

Chapter Fourteen

Dread Hollow Road
Saturday, May 6, 7:00 a.m.

Tara placed her weapon into her holster, checked her utility belt. She was set.

She hustled down the stairs, noting that her shoes were in need of a polish. No time now. When this case was wrapped up.

When Jacob's parents were safely back home.

This was day six since the couple went missing. No ransom demand. No nothing. Tara stared at the coffee machine. Six days was too long. They could already be dead. She didn't want to think that way, but her training wouldn't allow her to pretend. As much as she wanted to believe in the power of prayer and hope, she had to be realistic. Jacob was counting on her and she couldn't fail to find the truth. But she also couldn't fail to be straight with him. The truth might not be what he wanted to hear.

If there were no leads or news by the end of the

day, she and the kid were going to have to have an unpleasant conversation. She had to prepare him for the reality that this might not end well.

Whatever the reason, his parents had disappeared. If whoever took them didn't want anything in exchange for their safe release, then the abduction was about revenge or punishment for some boundary crossed.

Tara poured coffee into her travel mug and turned off the coffee maker. She grabbed the piece of toast she'd popped in when she started the coffee maker and tucked it between her teeth. She would eat on the way. Almost forgetting, she grabbed the tin of cookies as well. Before going to the office, she intended to check in at the house on Falling Rock Trace. Hanson hadn't given her an update this morning. She had a right to know what was happening in her town.

She opened the door and came face-to-face with Deke. She almost choked on a startled gasp; her teeth pushed through the dry toast and all but the one bite hit the floor.

Deke grimaced. "You call that breakfast?"

She chewed. Swallowed. Downed a swig of too hot coffee. Groaned. "I didn't have anything in the fridge."

Deke held up a bag. "I stopped by the diner. Delilah said you need to eat."

The scent of bacon and eggs on homemade biscuits teased her senses. She grabbed the bag. "Thanks. I really have to go."

"Five minutes," he argued, his hands up like a crossing guard's. "You can sit down and eat. Five minutes."

Big breath. "You're right. Okay." She did an about-face and took a seat at her table. "There's more coffee in the carafe." He knew his way around her kitchen. No need to give him directions.

The way he'd taken her to the edge last night with nothing but that deep voice and sweet words flashed in her mind, heated her cheeks. She tore into the bag. Found two loaded biscuits. She placed one on the other side of the table, at the seat farthest from her. Then she unwrapped her sandwich and took a bite. Her eyes closed and she savored the taste of Delilah's amazing ability to create an explosion in the taste buds. The woman should have her own cooking show.

"I hope you managed some sleep last night."

"Slept like a rock." Which was a miracle considering she'd found human and pet remains. She'd made no major headway on her case. Not to mention this case had caused her to allow Deke way too close.

"I couldn't sleep." He bit into his biscuit.

She felt guilty for not considering how worried he was about Jacob. The boy was his student. He was close to the kid.

"This is hard for you. You've spent a lot of time with Jacob. Your students are like extended family." He'd said as much when they were together.

He reached for his coffee. "I wish I could protect them all. Teachers see lots of good things. The joy of

watching the children bloom academically and so-
cially. But we also see the bad. The abuse. The painful medical issues. And times like this when they
lose a person or people they love and depend upon."

"It's a tough job," she agreed. "Every bit as tough
as being a cop. You protect and serve just as we do."
She smiled. "Your weapon is the power of knowledge."

"You know how to make a guy feel special." He
finished off his biscuit.

That smile. His eyes. They were too familiar. Too
able to slip deep inside her and make her want things
she shouldn't want.

"Thanks for the breakfast, but I really have to go."

Their cells sounded off simultaneously. Her call
was from Collin.

"Hey," Deke said in greeting to his caller.

Tara moved away from the table. "What's up? I'm
heading in now."

"Ms. Wright just called the station," Collin said
in a rush.

"When?" Deke said, his voice taut.

Tara tried focusing on her call, but the pallor that
had slid over Deke's face had her needing to hear
his conversation.

"Jacob is missing," Collin said.

"What?" Tara's attention zeroed in on his voice.
"Missing?"

"I'm on my way," Deke said. His call ended.

"When Ms. Wright went to wake him, his bed was

empty. She thinks he's been gone for a bit because the sheets were cold."

"Heading there now," Tara said, "meet me." She ended the call and met Deke's gaze. "I'll drive."

They rushed out of the house. Loaded up and roared out of her driveway.

"What did Ms. Wright tell you?" Tara knew without asking that she would have called Deke right after calling the police.

He repeated the same thing Collin had told Tara in his call.

"Why would he run away?" Deke shifted, turning his body toward her. "Would the people who took his parents come back for him after six days?"

"I don't know." Tara wished she could provide a different answer, but she couldn't say what she didn't know. "Going to the cave may have triggered fears we didn't recognize."

"Surely he wouldn't try to get back to the cave." Deke stared out the window. His face told her he felt sick at the idea of Jacob out there somewhere in trouble.

"For now," Tara said gently, "we'll have a close look at the Wright home to ensure she didn't overlook anything. We'll go from there."

The steps she would need to take whizzed through her head. Amber Alert. Damn.

Jacob, where are you?

Five endless minutes later, they arrived at the

Wright residence. Collin was there already. He and Ms. Wright were in the front yard talking.

Tara and Deke exited her vehicle and joined them.

Wright swiped at her eyes. "I can't believe he would run away on his own. He's been so sweet and respectful all week."

"What time did you put him to bed?" Tara asked.

"As soon as Deke brought him back. Since they'd stopped for pizza and ice cream, I ushered him into the bath and then we tucked him into bed. It was maybe ten or ten fifteen. I checked in on him before I went to bed, and he was fast asleep. We all crashed pretty early." She shook her head. "I can't believe Ben and I slept through whatever happened. We're usually hyper aware of every little sound."

Ben Wright was her husband. Whoever had broken in had been particularly quiet not to wake anyone in the household, not even the dogs.

"What about Jelly Bug?" Deke asked.

"The dog is gone too," Wright explained.

Tara turned to Collin. "I'll have a look in the room. Start talking to neighbors. See if anyone saw or heard anything."

"On it."

Collin headed next door and Tara turned back to Wright. "Can you or your husband help with talking to neighbors until we can assemble a search party?"

"Ben will stay here. I need to be the one helping." Tears welled in her eyes once more. "I feel like this is my fault."

Tara gave her a quick hug. "This is not your fault. Now, let's find him." She shifted to Deke. "Come with me."

They entered the house. The Wright child was on the sofa next to his dad. They both looked worried.

"I need to have a look in the room where Jacob was sleeping."

Mr. Wright nodded. "First door on the left."

Tara followed the hall to the row of bedrooms. Two on the front side of the house. A third on the back side as well as the family bathroom.

The covers were turned down on the bed. Since no pj's lay on the floor or on the bed, Tara assumed he'd left with those on. "We need a description of what he was wearing."

A gentle whisper of air moved the window curtain. Tara looked up to the ceiling, no ceiling fan, and then down to the floor near the window for a central heating and air register. The register was on the floor right under the window. She moved close enough to check for air movement. Nothing. She moved aside the curtain.

The window was open just a crack. The screen had been removed.

"He went out the window."

Deke moved closer to her.

"Don't touch the window." She turned away from the obvious exit point. "I need to secure this room."

The next few minutes were a whir of activity. Collin returned to the house to lift prints from the window and the screen that had been placed on the ground outside the house. He would seal off the room for now. Tara issued an Amber Alert for Jacob, then said a quick prayer.

Within the hour they had dozens of volunteers gathered for starting a search. Tara left Collin in charge of coordinating the volunteers. She needed to check Jacob's house and the cave on Falling Rock Trace. Granted, she couldn't imagine how he would have gotten there. That said, after his reaction yesterday, it was necessary to rule out the location.

Wright had confirmed that Jacob had been wearing Spider-Man pajamas. Her son's bicycle was still at the house, so if he hadn't left the house with someone, he'd left on foot. If that was the case, Tara hoped he would come to his senses and knock on a door for help.

Tara slid behind the wheel of her Wagoneer, and Deke climbed into the passenger seat. They drove first to Jacob's house. Checked inside. Checked the yard. Nothing. It took only a few minutes more to check with the neighbors. No one had seen Jacob.

From there they headed to Falling Rock Trace.

"Someone took him," Deke said after several minutes of silence. "Jacob is too smart to take off like this."

Since it hadn't rained in days, there were no footprints anywhere in the Wright's backyard. Not that she'd expected to find any in that lush lawn. So far, none of the close neighbors had exterior video cameras of any sort.

"I'm with you on that," Tara said. "It's possible the perps came back for Jacob for leverage if the parents aren't cooperating."

"It took them six days to reach that point?" Deke said, incredulous.

"It doesn't make sense," Tara agreed. "I'm tossing out scenarios. Your job is to find the flaw in the reasoning."

"I can do that."

She glanced at him. Grateful he was calming down a bit. "I'm certain you can."

"What else you got?"

"Is it possible Jacob hasn't told us everything from Sunday night or from before his parents went missing?" The idea had nudged Tara, but the boy seemed sincere. Still, he was a kid. Kids lacked the reasoning skills that maturity would bring. If his father or mother asked him to keep a secret, he likely would. Like the one about the cave.

"My gut says he isn't keeping anything from us," Deke said. "But you're right. He may feel like he's protecting his parents. Although I can't imagine his mother doing such a thing, they could have stolen money from some drug lord and he's afraid to tell you they committed a crime."

"That's what worries me." Tara gripped the steering wheel tighter. "If he ran away this morning or last night, then my guess is he's hiding something."

"If someone took him…" Deke began, his words trailing off.

"Then he's in trouble because there's only one reason for a bad guy to come after a kid when he already has the adults."

"Leverage."

"Yes."

The silence that followed was thick with worry.

Official vehicles sat in the grass and along the road at the bone house. She spotted Hanson's vehicle right away. As they walked toward the house, suited techs came out carrying evidence boxes.

"I guess Hanson hit a gold mine." She hadn't seen anything particularly relevant other than the photo. Then again, she hadn't searched the closets and drawers. Or the attic. For all she knew, there could have been loads of evidence in the crawlspace. None of that mattered to her just now. Finding Jacob was her only priority.

At the door, she selected shoe covers and gloves from the box left on the porch. Deke did the same. They wandered in, found Hanson in the kitchen. He didn't look particularly happy to see them.

Before Hanson could chastise her for entering his crime scene with a civilian, she said, "Jacob Callaway went missing sometime during the night. We need to have a look around outside and in the woods to make sure he didn't come here."

"I'm sorry to hear that. Feel free to search anywhere on the property except in here. The house is off-limits."

"Thanks."

She had nothing else to share with him and he clearly didn't intend to share anything with her. Deke followed her back into the yard.

"I don't like that guy."

"Nobody does."

They headed for the tree line. Thankfully, this time they weren't lunging through the brush and darting around trees.

Tara's cell phone sounded off. She desperately hoped it was Collin with good news. Her father's face flashed on the screen. Disappointment speared her. Guilt followed. She loved her dad. It just wasn't a good time. "Hey, Dad."

She flashed a smile at Deke as her steps slowed.

"I just saw the news about human remains being found. What's going on?"

"I don't know a lot," she said. "The first of those three houses on Falling Rock Trace. Small brick rancher. We were in the area searching for anyone who had hired Jeff Callaway for odd jobs like landscaping."

"I know the area. Let's see…" He hummed a moment while he dredged the memory that failed him all too often. "Kosh—Ed and his wife, and the newer folks, Partons, I think. The other house was a woman. Something…"

Tara didn't give him the answer. Doing so would

only frustrate him. Instead, she waited. Kept moving forward, avoiding trees and the thicker areas of brush.

"Grant. You know, like the sunglasses back when I was a younger man."

Tara smiled, thankful he'd managed. "We haven't confirmed, but we believe her name was Melanie Grant. Not my case though. Our friendly FBI agent swooped in and took over the scene. He believes it's connected to the old Treat Foster case."

"I always hated when that happened." He exhaled a big breath. "Tell Deke we're still on for tomorrow's game. You should come. We can all have lunch together."

"I'll tell him." She hesitated. Hated to do what she had to do next. "Look, Dad, I hate to cut the call short, but Jacob Callaway has disappeared on us. He either ran away or someone took him. Deke and I as well as dozens of volunteers are out looking for him now."

"Good Lord. Let me know when you find him. You got this, sweetie. Love you."

"Love you too." Tara put her phone away, wished she could stop the disease stealing her father away.

"He's doing well, considering," Deke said, reading her mind.

She nodded, fought the burn of tears. Damn it.

"I was wondering," he said, when she didn't say more, "you think it's strange Jelly Bug is missing too?"

"Not at all. The dog would likely have barked if

Jacob had gone out that window leaving her there. He—meaning the perp—wouldn't have wanted to risk waking the Wrights."

"Could be a woman," Deke offered. "A woman would have an easier time manipulating Jacob."

"Another good point." She shot him a smile. "If you ever decide to give up teaching, you'd make a great cop."

He laughed. "I'll stick with what I love."

She parted a thicket and eased through. "Smart move," she agreed.

They reached the cave opening and Deke insisted on going inside first.

"Keep in mind," she said as she gingerly moved across the rocks, "I'm the one with the gun."

He paused. "Good point." Then he grinned. "Stay behind me."

Always the chivalrous one. In this case, maybe to a fault.

The cave was just as damp and dank as before. No sign of Jacob or Jelly Bug.

To cover all bases, they decided to call his name repeatedly as they made their way back to the house. Even if Jacob wouldn't answer, Jelly Bug would probably bark.

Tara called his name until she felt hoarse. Deke echoed her every call. No response. No barking.

Hanson was waiting outside when they reached the tree line. "No luck?"

Tara shook her head. "It was a longshot that we'd

find him here, but we had to be sure. I'd appreciate it if you'd keep an eye out for the boy and let me know if you see or hear anything that might help our search for him and his parents."

"Sure thing."

Somehow his assurance didn't give her much comfort.

When they were back on the road, Deke asked, "Where to now?"

"I'll check in with Collin. We'll fill in wherever we're needed."

"Can we swing by my house?"

"Of course." She divided her attention between him and the road. "You think he'd go looking for you?"

"It's worth a shot. I mean, I didn't check around the yard or garage when I left this morning."

"I keep thinking there was something I should have said to him last night," Tara offered, "to reassure him. Maybe this wouldn't have happened."

"If someone gave him a ride, and we know that's what happened, nothing you failed to say is why he's missing."

Deke was right. She knew this, but she felt sick anyway.

Silence simmered for a minute.

"Is there something I didn't say or do that made you go?"

How could he bring that up now?

"Deke."

"Just tell me so I can stop making a fool out of

myself." He stared at her profile, making the moment even more uncomfortable. "What did I do?"

"It wasn't and isn't you," she said, frustrated. "It's me."

"Come on. That's a cop-out. There has to be a reason that involves both of us. It can't be just you."

"I'm sorry to disappoint you, but you're wrong. It's me. Only me. You're an amazing man, Deke. Good looking, great personality. Dedicated to your work. It's not you. You can take your pick of the available women anywhere, and whatever happens, the problem will never be you."

She braked to a stop and shifted into Park.

"You do still have feelings for me."

She closed her eyes and reached for patience. "Deke."

"Tell me I'm wrong." He stared at her, his gaze searing right through her skin. "I need to hear something real…something good right now."

She released her seat belt and turned to him. She understood. The feeling of helplessness was overwhelming. "I have feelings for you. I want to be your friend, but we can't go there because you are stuck in this other place that we can't be anymore."

He tugged his seat belt loose. "Double talk. Just say it. You have feelings for me. The same feelings I have for you. You just refuse to admit it."

Tara got out. She wasn't dealing with that right now.

"I rest my case," he said, following her.

Without saying a word, they checked the garage

and the shed. Walked down to the lake and had a look around. Called his name.

No Jacob. No Jelly Bug.

Collin called. He had nothing either.

Tara's gut was in knots. Where the hell were these people? What the hell had they done?

"We should rendezvous with Collin. Figure out the strategy from here."

Deke said nothing. Climbed into the passenger side of her vehicle. She settled behind the wheel and started the engine.

No one vanished into thin air.

She suddenly had this awful feeling that the answer was right in front of her.

The simplest answer was usually the right one.

All she had to do was clear away all the clutter and static.

And find Jacob.

Chapter Fifteen

1:00 p.m.

Deke had started to sweat. Not from the heat, and it was unseasonably warm for early May, but because they'd found nothing on Jacob.

No reports of anyone having seen him. No breadcrumbs to suggest where he'd gone. Not one damned thing.

He felt sick. How had he spent five days a week this entire school term in the classroom with Jacob and not recognized something was going on with his family? Last fall when his mother was so sick, Deke had visited the family. He'd rallied the parents of other students in the class to help the family with meals. More than a few had made significant donations.

But everything had appeared to turn around by early this year. By February his mom was working again. Jacob was back to wearing his characteristic big smiles. Deke had spent some time last night mulling over what he knew of Jeff and Krissy Callaway. Good people. Earnest people. He couldn't see either one of them getting involved with criminals.

Except desperation and fear changed the best of folks.

"Let's load up and head to the school." Tara's voice dragged him from the gut-wrenching thoughts.

"Is it normal not to get any hits on an alert?" All the television crime shows always showed an abundance of information coming in when the police asked for help from the community. They'd gotten nothing on Jacob this morning. It was past noon, and they'd found the same. Nothing.

"This is a small community. We're not going to get a lot of false leads in an area this small where everyone knows everyone else. Eventually the bizarre ones and even plenty of sincere ones that turn out to be not connected to Jacob will trickle in from the larger communities."

Deke paused at the front end of her Wagoneer. "You think this is going to turn into the latter?"

The uncertainty on her face gave him the answer before she spoke. "I hope not."

They drove to the school without talking. Deke wasn't sure he could open his mouth again without being sick. Not something he cared to do in Tara's presence. She had always seen him as strong and tough. With a kid missing, he wasn't feeling nearly strong or tough enough.

She pulled into the parking lot at the gym. Dozens

of other cars were already there. This much support from the community buoyed his hopes. They made their way to the gym and as he'd expected judging by the number of vehicles in the lot, the crowd was pretty big. The smell of hamburgers and French fries had his stomach rumbling.

"Look," Tara said, pointing up ahead, "Delilah's got her crew from the diner serving food."

This was just one of the reasons Deke loved the Hollow. For a place associated with hauntings and eerie goings-on, the people were amazing, good and kind.

He and Tara queued up in the line for food. It was a necessary break. The search could go on the rest of the day...or for the next several days. Staying hydrated and energized for activity was important. Jacob was depending on them to find him and his folks.

Once they were seated on the bleachers, Collin joined them, and he and Tara went over where they were with the search and incoming tips.

"Patricia called me," Collin said before taking a draw from his drink.

Deke had met Collin's wife. Nice lady. A little on the odd side.

Tara said, "The kids okay?"

"They are. She says wherever Jacob and his parents are, it's dark."

Tara frowned. "Like in a cave?"

Deke immediately thought of the cave on Falling Rock Trace.

Collin shrugged. "Dunno. She just said it's dark. They're okay, but it's dark and they're scared."

"Thank her for the info," Tara said. "If you hear anything else from her, let me know. Right now, I'll take any tips I can get."

Collin nodded at Deke. "She's the real thing."

Deke gave a nod. Like Tara, he didn't care where the tips came from, he just wanted them to keep coming.

From the moment Tara issued the alert, the Sheriff's Department quickly sent out the information and readied a staff to take incoming calls and information, all of which would be forwarded to Tara and Collin in the field. More deputies had arrived to help. Hamilton County Sheriff's Department uniforms were sprinkled throughout the crowd in the gym.

Deke forced himself to take a bite of his burger. It tasted good, like everything else Delilah prepared, but it was difficult to enjoy the food. He ate for fuel.

Tara picked at her fries. Nibbled at her burger. Finally, she set her paper plate aside and turned to Deke. "It's time for the briefing. This won't take long and then we're back out there in the search."

He nodded, forced another bite.

Tara and Collin moved to a higher level on the bleachers and called the crowd to attention. Taking turns as if they'd practiced for this moment, they explained the lack of leads, which very well could indicate Jacob was still close, adding another layer of urgency to the local search. If he was close, he might not be for long. Tara encouraged the volunteers to finish up with the break and grab a new assignment at the table by the door. Tom Collier, a retired local deputy and avid researcher of Dread Hollow history, had volunteered to map out grid areas for the searchers. With his wife at his side, they would be handing out assignments to groups of ten.

It still amazed Deke how they'd pulled this together so quickly. He was immensely grateful.

When the briefing was finished, he and Tara followed the crowd to the table at the exit. Collier had laid out the remaining areas of the Hollow into ten manageable sections. He used a larger map to indicate each section. Smaller maps would be given to the groups.

The groups already working together split off, the group leaders coming forward one by one to accept assignments.

The group Deke and Tara joined had Scarlett Peterson from the library as their leader. Tara and Collin might have to break away at any moment, so they didn't take leader roles in any of the groups. Smart move in Deke's opinion.

With surprising speed, the groups filtered out of the gym.

Deke walked alongside Tara, still marveling at how quickly all these steps had been set in motion.

Tara paused at the driver's-side door of the Wagoneer and took a call. "Hey, Dad, what's going on?"

Deke waited on the opposite side of the hood before getting in. If her father was calling, he'd either heard something or thought of something helpful.

Deke was game for either.

"We'll be right there," Tara assured. She tucked her phone away. "Dad says he has some information he wants to show us. He believes it's relevant to what's going on with Jacob and his family."

"We heading to Forrest Hills?"

"Yeah. He says he has it all laid out for us."

"Let's go."

Hope pushed into Deke's chest. It was the first he'd experienced all morning.

Tara navigated out of the parking lot and onto Main Street. "Let's be prepared for the possibility this may be a theory the less-reliable part of his brain has created."

Deke understood. Her father was fine—or so it seemed—but sometimes he went off on a tangent that made no sense whatsoever.

"There's a lot of memories about the Hollow stored in that man's head," Deke said. "If we're lucky, he's tapped into something no one else has thought of or has reason to know."

From the stories Tara had told Deke, Tarrence Norwood had handled people and situations a little differently than most sheriffs. He used his own judgement at times rather than following the letter of the law. Deke could see him doing that. He was a good man, a fair man and sometimes the law left no room for mercy.

"He's very fond of you," she said as she made the turn onto Dread Hollow Road that would take them to Forrest Hills.

She didn't look at him when she made the statement.

Was she afraid of what he'd see in her eyes? Though she fought the idea, he was well aware she still wanted him on some level. He intended to fuel that want every chance he got.

"I'm fond of him." Deke grinned to himself. Another first for the day. "I'm fond of you too." He thought of their conversation late last night. "I apologize for going too far with my call. I guess I got a little excited."

A little? Hell, he'd lost all control. He wouldn't tell her what he'd had to do when that call ended. It was either take matters in his own hands or snap.

She cleared her throat. "Apology accepted."

He watched her. Studied the way she moistened her lips and blinked a couple of times as if recalling something she didn't really want to remember.

"You didn't get excited?"

She turned into the parking area of Forrest Hills. "I have no idea what you're talking about."

"You were breathing pretty fast. Getting a little heated maybe."

She shoved into Park and glared at him, her cheeks red with something like indignation. "That was frustration you heard. And the only heat I felt was anger at your inappropriate remarks."

Now she was mad.

"Sorry. I couldn't help myself."

"I'm glad one of us was having fun."

She was out and marching toward the entrance before he could remove his seat belt. There he went again, shoving his whole foot into his mouth. In this case, he was mostly latching onto a distraction to prevent losing his mind.

He hustled to catch up with her. "You're right. I was being a jerk."

"You were. That call was way out of line."

"I meant just now," he said. "I don't regret the call, just the pushing boundaries part."

She paused at the door, stared up at him. "Just remember, payback can be a bitch."

She opened the door and stormed inside.

Stunned, he watched. The door closed in front of him, snapping him out of his trance. He rushed after her.

When they'd signed in at the desk and walked on, he asked, for her ears only, "What does that mean?"

She kept moving, making the turns in the corridor that would lead to her father's apartment. "You'll see."

He wasn't sure whether to be excited or worried.

She knocked on the door and it opened. Her dad waved them inside. "Wait until you see what I've figured out."

He had cleared his model-assembling tools from

the table and spread pages on it. His laptop sat in the middle, the screen open to an online article.

"What's all this?" Tara asked.

"You told me on the phone about the house on Falling Rock Trace. The one you think is owned by Melanie Grant. You think the remains you discovered are hers."

Deke surveyed the pages as they spoke. Most were about Treat Foster.

"We haven't confirmed it yet," Tara reminded him, "but yes, that's where I'm leaning."

"You're probably right. Grant would be about eighty by now. Anyway, after you called, I couldn't stop thinking about her and that house."

Tara shared a glance with Deke, then asked her father, "Are you feeling okay, Dad?"

He waved her off. "I'm fine. Fine. Better than fine. Listen to me."

"Okay," Tara agreed.

"Long time ago, when I was just a deputy, I don't recall the exact year, but before I became sheriff..."

Deke watched him closely, noted the struggle with getting his words out that he'd never noticed before. Maybe it was only because the man was agitated, excited, whatever. But the idea of him struggling sent an ache through Deke.

"When I was just a kid," Tara offered.

He nodded. "You'd just had that princess birthday party."

There it was, the year. The princess birthday party

had been when Tara was two. Deke smiled. "She was a cute kid."

Her father's face softened. He relaxed. "She was." He blinked. "Anyway, I got a call from dispatch to go out to Falling Rock Trace. The house turned out to be the one where the recluse lived. That's what folks around here called her." He shrugged. "Some were unkind about her. She was a little strange. She rarely came into town, but when she did, she was often dressed in her housecoat and barefoot. Sometimes she'd wear nothing but a slip—the kind your mother wore under her dresses."

"She may have had a mental illness," Tara suggested.

Her father nodded. "She did. At the time, there were rumors she'd been in Moccasin Bend, but she wasn't listed as having been a patient. Maybe she had an alias. I can't say about that."

He reached for the laptop, pointed to the screen. "If you do a search on her name, nothing about her comes up. There are lots of Melanie Grants but not that Melanie Grant. I remember she didn't have a record. No family. It was like she was completely alone in this world."

At every pause, Tara waited patiently. Deke had to hold himself back from saying *and...?*

"So I went to her house that night. She'd called in about an intruder. When I arrived on the scene, there was no one there except her. She was wearing a dirty nightgown and her hair was a mess, like she hadn't combed it in weeks. She was very upset. Crying. I didn't smell any alcohol on her breath. I concluded that she was having an episode. I calmed her down and ushered her back into the house." He shook his head. "It was piled high with stuff. Like one of those people…hoarders. It was truly sad."

"You didn't find any signs of anyone having been there?" Tara asked.

He shook his head. "I checked every window, inside and out. I walked all around the yard, checked the tree line. Couldn't find a thing. Finally, she seemed satisfied that no one was about. She wanted tea." He laughed, a sad sound. "Of all things, the woman wanted me to make her tea. I rummaged through her cabinets and found an old box of the peppermint stuff. Little bags. Finding a clean cup was the hard part. Anyway, I made her tea—without the requested honey because she didn't have any. While she drank it, she told me she hadn't always been like that. I asked what she meant and she gestured to her dirty gown and the mess around her house."

He fell silent again. Deke and Tara shared a glance as they waited.

"She said her father abused her horribly. Her mother died when she was a kid and her father was a demon, for sure. She ran away from home when she was seventeen. Then every man she thought might love her only used her and tossed her away. By the time she was twenty, she found herself pregnant with no place to go. She tried her best to take care of the child, a girl named Gillian, but by the time the little girl was in school, it was no longer possible to hide her lack of ability, financially and otherwise, to care for the child. Social Services took her and she never saw the child again."

Deke knew that kind of story all too well and he hated it. "I'm sure she appreciated you listening to her story."

Mr. Norwood nodded. "She said she'd never told anyone before. From there, her life only got worse. It wasn't until she was forty and nearly starved to death that she found her brother. He'd run away the same time she did."

Beside Deke, Tara's breath caught. "Treat Foster."

Her father nodded. "He bought her that house on Falling Rock Trace. Course, I didn't have a clue who he was. She just called him T, like the letter, anyway. But now I know."

"How'd you figure it out?" Deke asked.

He lifted his hand and tapped a finger next to his eye. "The sunglasses."

Deke had no clue what he meant.

"When her brother ran away, he changed his name. Started a whole new life."

"His last name was originally Grant," Tara said knowingly. "He changed it to Foster. Foster Grant, the sunglasses you said were so popular when you were a kid."

Her father nodded. "The one and only. Anyway, when I asked how to contact him, she closed up like a turtle in its shell. I'm guessing he didn't want his past associated with his present. He was on his way up in the banking world."

"Thank you so much, Dad," Tara offered. "This helps tremendously. Jeff Callaway, Jacob's father, did work at the Grant home. If Treat Foster left some of the money he took with his sister, that would explain how Callaway came to have it."

"That's not the end of the story," her father said, his eyes gleaming.

"There's more?" Tara prompted.

He nodded. "She told me that night all those years ago that her brother helped her to find her daughter. Grant just wanted to make sure she was okay. And she was. The girl was living in Nashville at the time. Gillian Randall, her foster family had adopted her. She had gone to college and become an accountant. Grant's eyes just lit up when she talked about her, even though her daughter had asked her not to come back. Grant didn't hold that against her. She understood. She was just so thankful that her daughter had married a well-to-do young man by the name of James Hanson. He worked for the Tennessee Bureau of Investigations."

"Wait." Tara looked taken aback. "Hanson? James Hanson?"

"You got it. I just looked up James and Gillian Hanson. They have one child, a boy—well, a man now. He's an FBI agent assigned to the Chattanooga office."

Deke rallied from the shock. "The FBI guy! He has to know. He's at her house now." It wasn't likely the man was involved in the abductions. "He has to know the remains in that house probably belong to his biological grandmother."

"And," Tara said, her tone just shy of outrage, "he must be aware that Treat Foster is his biological uncle."

"Why the hell would he keep this from you when the Foster case connects to your missing persons case?" Deke asked.

"I'm sure he doesn't want to reveal his connection to Foster." She hugged her dad. "Thanks, this is incredibly helpful. I gotta go."

Deke gave her dad a nod and followed Tara into the corridor. "Are you planning to confront Hanson?"

"Damn straight, I am. He's guilty of a number of crimes already, obstruction in an ongoing investigation for one." She pushed through the exit doors and into the sun. "We have a nine-year-old boy missing. What the hell is Hanson thinking?"

Deke figured they were about to find out.

Chapter Sixteen

Falling Rock Trace, 3:00 p.m.

Tara felt furious. She took a curve faster than she'd intended. Her grip tightened on the wheel.

"You might want to slow down just a little," Deke pointed out.

She shot him a glare.

A skidding stop in front of the Grant house startled even her. When the rocking stopped, Deke dropped his hands from the dash, where he'd braced himself.

"We made it." He wrenched his door open, muttered under his breath, "Miraculously."

Tara ignored his jab and climbed out. She stalked toward the house, ignoring the new crime-scene tape and the white-clad techs coming in and out.

"May I help you, ma'am?"

She stopped just short of barreling into a well-polished suit—another fed no doubt.

"Deputy Sheriff Tara Norwood. I'm looking for Agent Hanson," she managed to demand. Her throat was tight with fury.

"I'm afraid he's not here, ma'am."

Beyond the agent, she could see just far enough inside to recognize they were taking the house apart, one wall at a time, down to the studs.

"Find anything yet?" she asked. She was aware Deke had joined her. He hovered right behind her, probably glaring at the guy.

"I'm afraid I'm not at liberty to say." The fed glanced at Deke.

"Where is Hanson?" she demanded. That she didn't shout was a sheer miracle.

"He needed some privacy for holding a teleconference. One of the other deputies went with him to let him into the substation."

A new blast of fury roared through her. "Thank you."

Deke had the good sense to step away just in time for her to stamp back to her vehicle. He pulled up the rear, climbing in as she started the engine.

"Maybe I should drive," he offered.

She didn't respond, just cut him a look that dared him to say it again.

When you knew a man the way she knew Deke Shepherd, you had earned the privilege not to mince words.

Drawing in a couple of calming breaths, she drove more judiciously to the substation. When she confronted Hanson, she needed to be calm and rational. It wouldn't be easy considering she had three missing persons, one being a child. She didn't have time for games.

"Thank you," Deke said when they parked.

She pulled in another breath. "Sorry. I was upset."

He bit back a grin. "I noticed."

Tara couldn't get out quickly enough. The door was locked; she unlocked it and stepped inside. Just because Hanson was a federal agent didn't mean he was allowed to bend the rules in Dread Hollow.

She heard his voice and followed it to the small conference room, which was really just another office. He spotted her and ended his call.

He closed up the notebook he'd been using and stood. "I hope you don't mind me using your conference room."

"Would it matter?"

His hands went into his pockets. "I suppose not." He glanced at Deke, who leaned in the doorway, arms crossed over his chest.

Deke looked angry as well. She was glad. She hoped he made Hanson uncomfortable.

"What's up?" Hanson had the audacity to ask.

Tara laughed, a very unpleasant sound. "You do realize I have two missing adults and as of this morning a missing child." This was not a question. He would have to be hiding in a cave somewhere with no cell service not to know. Bastard.

"Any progress on finding them? The Bureau can help if you're ready to go that route."

Wasn't he just the picture of helpfulness?

"Have you told your superiors about your personal connection to this case?"

He frowned but it didn't go deep. "Which case? Your case? I'm afraid I don't know what you mean."

"Lying never looks good on a lawman, Mr. FBI agent. There's only one case. *The* case that involves my missing persons and the legendary Treat Foster. The remains of the woman in the house was your maternal grandmother. She was the sister of Treat Foster. She is why there were rumors and all sorts of reports of people having seen him in this area before and even a few after his unexpected departure from his life."

Hanson dropped back into the chair he'd vacated upon her arrival. "How'd you figure it out?"

She pulled out a chair at the table and sat. "Are you seriously asking me that? What difference does it make? I know and I need to understand if and how any aspect of your grandmother's case is related to my missing persons."

Hanson glanced at Deke, who remained in the doorway.

"You can say whatever it is you have to say in front of him," Tara said. "He already knows anyway."

"I never met her, obviously," he said. "I didn't know about her until my mother's sixtieth birthday a couple of years ago. I planned to surprise her one afternoon, and I found her crying, staring at a photograph of a woman and a child. My mother explained that the child was her when she was eight. It was the last photo she had of her real mother."

"Did she not know her mother was in Dread Hollow?" Tara hated that she felt sympathy for him. Then again, maybe it was for his mother and grandmother.

"She did. She said her mother came to see her once, when I was just a toddler, thirty-two years ago."

It was difficult to imagine Hanson as a toddler. But everyone was a toddler at one time, even FBI agents.

"Her mother had heard about me and wanted to see her grandchild. She hoped to make amends with my mother, but Mother was having none of that. That day, when I found her crying, she admitted that she wished she had. But at the time all she saw was a haggard old woman who hadn't taken care of her who looked like a prison escapee. So she sent her away. Told her to never come back."

"You weren't curious about her?" Curiosity had often gotten Tara into trouble, but she could never help herself.

"A little at first, but my mother begged me never to contact her. She really didn't want me to know about her childhood. It was really awful. Abuse. Starvation. You name it. I couldn't go against her wishes. I couldn't hurt her that way."

Wow. The guy had a heart after all.

"If it means anything," Tara offered, "I would have done the same."

He gave her a nod. "I had no idea there was any sort of connection to the Treat Foster case. What agent wouldn't want to solve that one? It's a legend-ary black spot on the local field office's record."

"How did you find out?"

"When you found the money. The name and case popped up. I noted that it was in Dread Hollow, the place where Melanie Grant lived. Knowing how small the town was, I couldn't help wondering if she had known him. She had moved here just before he disappeared, I learned, and there were reports he'd been seen here. I mentioned it to my mother, and she said she couldn't be sure, but she thought he and her mother were somehow related. She'd heard her mother mention someone named Treat, but she never imagined they were siblings."

"But you figured it out after you came down here and took over my case."

He nodded. "I asked for the assignment to check up on where the money came from, and when you discovered her house and the remains, I started dig-ging. My mother never knew exactly where she lived or even if she was still alive. She only knew she lived in this area."

"Did you find anything that relates to the Calla-ways?" Tara needed a break on this case. Damn it.

"We found prints where Jeff Calloway had been in the house, at least as far as the bedroom door. I think he probably saw the remains and got the hell out. I can't say for sure. If the money was in her house, it's all that was there. We haven't found anything else. I did find a man's shirt that I'm thinking may have been Treat Foster's. There's no way to know for sure. She had files and notes about the purchase of the house and the furnishings. However they reconnected, it was before he took the money and walked away. I'm assuming he used his personal funds to buy the house."

"Based on the prescription bottles I saw, she was ill around the time Foster made his big exit." It was so strange that the dates and drug names were on the bottles but not the physician's or the patient's. Sounded fishy to Tara.

"It appears that way. My medical examiner has given me a preliminary time of death and it works with that timeline. He may have stayed with her while she was dying. Again, I'm speculating. As far as the money he took, it was from only three accounts. I have found letters written to the men who owned those accounts. It seemed each one—at different times in her life—carried on an affair with Grant and left her heartbroken. In her letters, it sounded as if the men were particularly abusive. Based on what she suffered at the hands of her own father, I can see how she would be particularly damaged by what happened."

"You think she told Foster while he was caring for her and he took his revenge on the three?" An interesting way to do so.

"Again, the timing works. He would have learned this information about six months before he took the money. Just before that, his wife had left him for his best friend. He may have had a crisis of some sort and sought out the only family he had. At least that's what my training as a profiler tells me."

"Bottom line," Tara concluded, "Melanie Grant and Treat Foster couldn't have given the money to Jeff Callaway."

"You're assuming," Hanson suggested, "that Foster is dead. We've found no other remains."

Deke moved into the room and sat down next to Tara as she asked, "Are you saying he could still be alive?"

"It's not impossible," Hanson said. "He would be in his eighties. Then again, he may have taken whatever portion of the money was left after Grant died and moved to the Cayman Islands or some other faraway place where we have no extradition treaty."

"Have you checked the caves?" This from Deke.

"Caves?" Hanson shook his head. "I don't know what you mean?"

"In the woods behind the Grant house," Deke explained, "there are caves. Deep caves with lots of twists and turns."

The idea of just how deep those caves could be struck Tara. "What if…" She turned to Deke, considered a moment before speaking the thought aloud in front of Hanson. What the hell? At this point, they needed to work together. "What if the Callaways are hiding deep in that cave somewhere? Or they were restrained there by the thugs who took them. If Jacob was taken to his parents, he would be there too."

Deke's face lit with the idea. "They may be waiting out the feds to see if they find more of the money." He glanced at Hanson. "No offense."

Hanson held up his hands. "None taken. But about these caves, we need to see them. Can you take me there?"

"We can." Tara stood. "You want to ride with us?"

Hanson grabbed his keys. "I'll follow you to the house."

"Sounds good."

Outside, Tara said, "Heads up." She pitched her keys to Deke. "How about you drive?"

He caught the keys. "I was only kidding before."

"I need to make some calls. You should drive."

They climbed in and headed for Falling Rock Trace.

First, Tara called Collin to brief him and find out if there was any news. There wasn't, of course. He would have called if any of the search teams had found anything. Next, she checked in with the department about the incoming calls she'd noticed. She received text alerts letting her know calls were coming in. Unfortunately, none panned out enough to even be pitched to Tara or Collin.

By the time she put her cell away, they had arrived at the Grant home. They climbed out and met Hanson in the driveway.

"Lead the way," he said.

Tara looked him up and down. "You sure you want to go into the woods in that suit?"

He laughed. "It's my uniform. Why not?"

Tara shrugged. "I can understand that."

Deke led the way. Five minutes of picking through brush and saplings and around trees and they were at the cave.

"This is the one," Tara told Hanson, "Jacob's father showed him when they came here for him to cut the grass."

"One of the neighbors," Hanson said, "a guy named Parton, said the other neighbor had kept the property cleaned up to avoid living on the same road with an eyesore."

"Right." Tara nodded. "I spoke to him as well. Based on what you've told me, I assume Callaway found the money and used it for his wife's medical expenses."

"Except for the $50K you found under the bed," Hanson pointed out.

Tara shrugged. "Except for that." She wasn't ready to label Callaway a bad guy. One who had made a grave error, she had decided.

"The Callaways are good people," Deke said, a warning in his voice. "If he took the money, it was out of desperation."

Hanson shrugged. "Maybe so, but robbery is robbery."

Deke looked ready to fight the guy, but instead he took Tara's flashlight and entered the cave. Tara stayed close behind him. Hanson brought up the rear.

The cave wasn't very wide at first. But after a

few yards, it made a turn that widened to a fairly large size. The journey had been at a downhill trajectory, which made the ceiling higher and higher. The deeper they went, the higher the ceiling.

As they reached the end of the corridor, another rock corridor, this one quite narrow, ventured off to the left.

Since Hanson had brought his own flashlight, they were able to get a better look around the larger area. There were definite signs someone had camped here, though not recently.

"We should check out the other corridor," Tara said.

Again, Deke took the lead. It was necessary to move forward single file. At some points, even slipping through sideways put Tara's nose too close to the rock in front of her. This was why she wasn't a spelunker.

No one talked. There was a feeling that there wasn't enough air. Claustrophobia, Tara suspected.

When they moved into a larger stone room, Tara sagged with relief. This one too was a dead end, it seemed. Not as large as the first one but maybe twelve by twelve. The idea that nature had formed all these spaces was awe-inspiring.

Hanson and Deke slowly roved their lights over the walls. The ceiling was lower here. Just a foot or so above their heads. The air seemed thick and smelled like dirt.

"Here we go," Deke announced. He backed up his

light and roamed the beam over what appeared to be clothing.

They all moved closer. There were canned goods. The pop-top kind. Boxes of crackers and cookies. The print on the boxes was barely readable. A few feet away from the food stockpile was evidence of a campfire.

"Have a look at this," Hanson said, his voice oddly dull.

Tara and Deke moved closer to his position.

His light had settled on a decaying quilt and a human skull.

Hanson passed his light to Tara and pulled on a pair of gloves. He drew back the quilt, which basically fell apart as he did, and surveyed the remains. A full skeleton. The clothes were in the same condition as the quilt, falling apart. Around the right wrist bones was a gold watch.

Hanson leaned closer. "Rolex."

"They have serial numbers," Tara pointed out.

"You're right," Hanson said as he pulled the watch free from the bones. He studied the watch before placing it into his jacket pocket. "One of Foster's colleagues at the bank said he bought himself a Rolex after his wife left him. I'd lay odds on this being it."

"I think you'd win that one," Deke said.

They searched the area for a while longer. Discovered more of the long-time missing money in a plastic bag. The money was in a shoebox tucked into the bag. Fifty thousand dollars. On the opposite side of what Tara couldn't help thinking of as a stone crypt, there were two more shoeboxes filled with cash.

"I believe," Tara said, "your case is solved, Agent Hanson."

He nodded. "I think you're right."

But none of this explained where Jacob Callaway and his parents were and what kind of trouble they'd gotten themselves into.

Chapter Seventeen

Dread Hollow Road, 9:00 p.m.

The search had been called off for the day, but Tara wasn't finished yet. She did, however, have to change shoes. She sat on her bedside. She held her breath as she pulled off first one shoe and then the other. She rolled off the sock on her left foot and winced at the blisters there.

She groaned. "You really screwed up today," she grumbled. She should have worn her sneakers for the search. Wearing her uniform hadn't been necessary and yet she had. "Ugh." And she'd thought Hanson was a fool for wearing his suit into the cave.

The other sock came off next. Her right foot had fared slightly better. She stood and hobbled across the hall to the upstairs bathroom.

"You okay up there?"

She closed her eyes and groaned again. "Yes. Go home, Deke. I'm going to take a shower and head back out."

She walked past the claw-foot tub she'd loved swimming in as a little kid. Her mom would laugh and clap her hands as Tara splashed around in the big old tub.

Another memory…one from the day her mother had died tried to intrude. Tara attempted to push it away, but failed. Her mother had been ill for a very long time and her father had taken care of her as well as any nurse. Nothing, not the call of his career or anything else, could have torn him away from her as long as she was still breathing. Tara had tried time and again to give him breaks but he refused to leave her. That day—the day she died—her mother had somehow emerged from the haze of pain medications long enough to smile and thank him for never allowing her to feel alone. That moment had made her father's sacrifice worth it. Had made Tara understand the meaning of true love.

Grabbing a towel as she passed the tiny closet, she made her way to the corner shower nook that was added when she was a teenager. She turned on the water. It would take a while to heat up, but she wasn't complaining. Other than the half bath downstairs, this was it. Folks hadn't clamored for three or more bathrooms when this house was built. Her father had grown up here as had her grandfather and great-grandfather and so on. Sadly, Tara would likely be the last of the Norwoods to live in this house. She was the last in her family. She closed her eyes and forced away those thoughts.

"Hey."

Her eyes flew open, and Deke stood in the doorway.

"I thought you went home!" she snapped. God, she was tired. Her feet were killing her. She was exhausted and her body complained that she needed to eat. The few bites of burger and fries she'd downed had been hours ago.

She hoped Jacob wasn't out there somewhere hungry. She closed her eyes and leaned against the nearest wall. Day six was ending, and they had nothing, N.O.T.H.I.N.G., on the missing family.

"Take your shower," Deke ordered. "I'll pull together something to eat. Then you're going to bed."

"Seriously?" She shook her head. "I do not intend to go to bed. I have calls to follow up on and I'm taking a drive around town. Past the school. Maybe out to Falling Rock Trace."

"Everyone," Deke said, daring to enter the room, "has gone home. Like you. Like me." He slapped his chest. "They are all exhausted. It's better to get some sleep and start fresh in the morning."

"The volunteers and you," she sent him a pointed look, "are not the deputy sheriff in charge of this community. I don't get to stop yet."

"Tara, I get that." He sank down onto the closed toilet lid. "But you shouldn't go back out tonight. You stay here and take care of the other stuff you have to do, and I'll take a drive around town, past the school and all that."

"Go," she ordered. "I can't do this right now."

She turned her back on him and started unbuttoning her shirt. To her surprise, he left the room, closing the door behind him. She striped off the uniform, slid her panties and bra off and stepped into the shower. The hot water beat against her skin instantly relaxing her muscles. She sagged against the wall.

She and Deke had spent way too much time together the past few days. She needed some time and space away from him before she did something totally reckless. Having sex with Deke would be awesome, no question. She hadn't been with anyone else since they ended their relationship.

Since you ended it.

If last night was any indication, she was badly in need of a round between the sheets. But she couldn't. It would be a mistake. The past six months had been far too difficult to take that kind of huge step backward.

She rubbed the soap over her skin, rinsed and took her time shaving, something she hadn't done in a week or more. Then she washed her hair. She stood beneath the water for a long while, enjoying the heat and steam. She needed it to cleanse her of all the troubling thoughts. She needed to relax.

But the haunting thoughts wouldn't go away.

Was Jacob okay?

What the hell had his parents gotten into? Had someone else learned about the money and wanted Callaway to take him or them to it?

What would she do if Deke came back tonight?

Don't think about it. He was off-limits. He'd promised to go.

Tara took her time, dried her hair and her body. She slathered lotion over her skin and then blew her hair dry. She sat on the toilet lid and attended to her blisters, adding salve to all and bandages to the worst ones. She checked her face in the mirror and decided she needed moisturizer there too.

Washed, dried and lotioned, she went to her room in search of a pair of comfy pj's. She dragged on clean underwear and the pink cotton pajamas she'd worn thin over the years. Next up was a thick pair of socks to pad her sore feet. Now to find her cell and respond to the dozens of text messages and several calls.

As she made her way along the upstairs hall, the smell of something amazing drifted up the stairs. Deke was supposed to leave, wasn't he?

What had he said? He'd drive around town while she took care of the things she needed to do? Right?

Whatever he'd said, someone was down there cooking and she would bet her beloved vintage Wagoneer that it was him.

Damn it.

She made her way down the stairs. Followed the smell of something delicious into her kitchen.

Deke closed the microwave and turned to place a serving bowl onto the table.

"What're you doing?" Hands on hips, she walked into the room.

"Heating up the food Delilah sent over."

Had Delilah been here? "I thought you were doing that drive around for me."

"I did. I drove down Main Street, past the library and the diner and around the school. I drove out to Jacob's house, got out and looked around. Then I drove out to Falling Rock Trace. I didn't see any sign of Jacob or his folks. When I headed back this way, Delilah called and said she had stew for us and that I should pick it up."

"Stew? For us?" It was a conspiracy. Tara was certain. Between her father and now Delilah, they were determined to throw Tara and Deke back together.

He stared at her patiently. "Sit. Eat. You'll feel better then."

She wanted to tell him that she wasn't going to sit and she wasn't going to eat, but she no longer had the wherewithal to fight that battle.

He ladled up a bowl of beef stew with root vegetables. It looked as good as it smelled. Delilah knew how Tara loved carrots and potatoes and parsnips.

She ate. Delilah would be hurt if she didn't eat. The fuel would help her brain function better. She needed to think clearly. To focus.

Deke filled his own bowl. Before sitting down, he went to the fridge and looked inside. He held up a carton of milk and a can of beer.

She gestured to the beer. He put the milk back and

grabbed a second beer. One he settled on the table in front of her, the other in front of his own bowl, then he sat down and started to eat.

Talk wasn't an option. At least not for Tara. She was too exhausted. Too overwhelmed to participate in even the simplest discourse. She wanted to eat and then to collapse into unconsciousness for a few hours. Setting her alarm for five in the morning would ensure she was up and ready to go by daylight.

When Tara could hold no more, she finished off her beer and carried her bowl to the sink. Deke passed his bowl to her and covered the leftover stew before stashing it in the fridge. It was a dance they'd shared many times before. Sometimes in this house. Sometimes in his cottage.

When she'd washed the dishes—this old farmhouse did not have a dishwasher—she turned to the man and tackled what she hoped would be the final hurdle of the evening. It had to be done. She couldn't deal with the tension any longer.

She leaned against the counter. "We can have sex if that's what you want?"

She'd decided to go the direct route.

The startled look on his face said she'd won the first round.

"What? That's not why I'm here."

"You don't want to have sex with me?" she demanded, laying on the pressure.

"Hell yes, I want to have sex with you." The fingers of one hand plowed through his hair, his gaze searching for some place to light on that didn't include looking at her.

"I've told you over and over that we can't go back to what we had, but we can have this—sex—if that's what you want. Friends with benefits, I guess."

He shook his head. "No. That's not what I want."

Her eyebrows flew upward. "Are you sure?"

"Tara, stop." Hands on hips now, he stared at her, his face a study in concern. "What're you doing?"

"I'm offering options. A long-term relationship is out, but there's always sex."

"You know that's not how I want it to be."

She stepped away from the sink, placed her hands on his chest and pushed them up and around his neck, enjoying the feel of hard muscle beneath his shirt. God, how she'd missed the feel of him.

"Kiss me," she ordered.

He reached for her hands to pull them away. "This is not going to work."

She tiptoed, brushed her lips against his. Felt his sharp intake of breath. "Isn't it?" she whispered.

His hands closed around her forearms. "Tara, I don't—"

She pressed her lips against his, cutting off his words. He held perfectly still for longer than she'd expected, but that didn't stop her. She pressed her body against his. Deepened the kiss. Traced her tongue over his lips.

He lost it then. His arms went around her and pulled her firmly against him. His body was hard and so damned warm. Hers melted into his. She lost herself to the feel of him. The scent of him.

A smart woman would stop this charade.

But she couldn't.

She hoped he would. Needed him to.

He lifted her onto the counter. Her legs spread instinctively, and he leaned into her. The layers of clothing separating them felt too confining. They needed to come off. She tried to pull her mouth from his, but she couldn't bear the loss. His lips slid away from hers, working down her throat. Her nipples peaked in anticipation of his mouth closing over them.

Her hands roved over his back. Against his neck and into his hair.

She warned herself again to stop. To pull away.

No way. No way.

He stilled. His forehead against her breastbone, his arms around her waist.

She did the same, her fingers buried in his hair. Her cheek against his head.

Their frantic breathing was the only sound in the room.

"Tara, I can't do this." He lifted his face to hers. "I want you more than you can know. But not like this. I want *all* of you."

The jolt of his words had her feeling ashamed that she'd started this and allowed it to go so far.

"You should go home. Please."

"I will. You have my word. I just need the truth. I need to know why. What did I do wrong?"

Delilah's voice…her father's voice echoed inside her.

"I allowed you too close," she confessed. "I made a mistake."

The haze of need still in his eyes and clouding his face, he said, "What does that mean?"

She leaned against the cabinets behind her and surrendered to the inevitable. "I told you my ex and I divorced over irreconcilable differences."

He moistened his lips. Nodded.

"The irreconcilable part was my round with cancer."

"What?"

"It was only a year after I moved back here to accept the position at the Sheriff's Department substation. I wanted the position to take advantage of the slower lifestyle and—at least until now—the lack of crime. We'd been married for a year, and I couldn't wait to start a family. But the cancer came first."

The pain in his eyes was like looking into a mirror and seeing what she felt. But he couldn't possibly feel this…emptiness.

"Tell me about the cancer," he said softly.

"I'd rather not go into the dirty details, but the bottom line is they had to take everything out. Uterus. Ovaries. There's nothing left." Her eyes burned with the emotion threatening. She forced it back. Would not cry. She'd had three years to get used to the idea of being barren. There was no excuse for tears at this point.

"You can't have a child." He stared directly into her eyes. "That's your issue?"

The urge to punch him was palpable. "Yeah. That's my issue. My ex wasn't interested in the new damaged me. So if you want all of me, that's what you get: No children."

She'd heard all the suggestions about surrogates and adoption and that just wasn't how she'd seen building her home. Besides it wasn't only her decision. The person with whom she'd spend the rest of her life would need to be in on the decision. So she'd bowed out. Opted not to bother.

Until this man crashed into her life. She'd been so alone. He'd been so sweet, so handsome, so damned perfect. She had foolishly fallen in love with him. Then reality had kicked her in the face and she'd had to pull out.

"There are other options."

She laughed. Couldn't help herself. "That's what people say when they're not in this position." She looked him square in the eyes now. "It sounds so easy right now, but what if those other options don't work out? Create other problems? You see, if we dive into this, you're not the one who doesn't have any other choices."

Some realization she couldn't fathom appeared to dawn on him.

"I get it. You're afraid in time I'll change my mind and leave you the way the other fool did."

Her heart thumped then sank. He'd hit the nail directly on the head. "He did and so will you. So would anyone who loves children as much as you do. This feeling of 'my barrenness doesn't matter' you're experiencing right now might not last. You can't be certain that you'll be satisfied with the other option. I don't want you to wish you'd made a different choice."

He nodded. "For the record, I'm no fool. But you're right." His hands dropped to the counter on either side of her thighs. "I do love children, but the fact is none of them are mine legally or biologically. More important, I love you. I'd love nothing more than to make babies with you. But if I have to choose between having babies and you, I choose *you*."

Her heart stumbled and she had to struggle to get a breath.

"You say that now," she argued, those damned tears charging onto her lashes, "but I'm left with the fallout when down the road you change your mind."

"I won't change my mind, Tara. If we decide we want the pitter-patter of little feet in our house, we'll adopt. There are lots of babies and kids out there who need a family to love them."

If only he'd stop saying all the right things.

Somewhere in the house, her cell sounded off. They both looked in the direction of the chime.

"I have to get that." She was already scooting from the counter.

Deke picked her up by the waist and stood her on the floor. She took off. She'd left the damned thing in the bathroom. She rushed up the stairs, her legs rubbery after making out with Deke, her heart torn after their talk.

She snatched up the phone just as it rang a final time before going to voice mail. "Deputy Norwood."

"Tara, it's me."

Brenda Wright.

"Is everything okay? Have you heard from Jacob?"

"No. No. But something has been bothering me all afternoon."

Tara sat down on the rolled top edge of the claw-foot tub. "Tell me what's going on."

"Last evening before Deke brought Jacob back, I had a visitor."

"Who?"

Deke was at the door now and Tara put the phone on speaker.

"Wilma Hambrick came by and raved on and on about how sad she was for poor Jacob. She'd been thinking about him all week. She brought over this lovely canister full of cookies for him. Peanut butter cookies. She said they were his favorite. I have no idea why she thought this. Jacob said he doesn't like peanut butter cookies, but we all love them. It was just odd. When Jacob came home that night, he passed on the cookies. Told me they were his least favorite. But we all ate at least one. I ate two. Even Jelly Bug had a cookie."

Tara wanted to say the effort was very nice of Wilma, but she suspected the other shoe was about to drop. "Go on," she urged.

"Today, after the lunch break, I was assigned to the search area that included her house. When I knocked on her door, she acted funny. She didn't even ask about Jacob, she just rushed me away with some excuse about her not feeling well. It was, I don't know, very strange. I told myself that maybe my appearance at her door was bad timing. Maybe she had a migraine. When I have one, I can't bear the light or to talk. But it has nagged at me since, and I just couldn't go to sleep without telling you."

All the times Hambrick had visited Tara and waxed on about how badly they needed a "real" police department fired in her brain like bullets. At this point, a lot of other folks were saying the same thing...but for different reasons. Three people were missing. Half a dozen or so burglaries had occurred in the past two weeks.

All of it adding to Hambrick's narrative.

How badly did the woman want to make this happen?

"Do you have any of those cookies left over?" Tara was up and moving past Deke and toward her bedroom, gesturing for him to follow. She handed the phone to him, and while Wright talked, Tara grabbed a sweatshirt from her closet, a pair of jeans and her sneakers.

"I think there's a few left over. The canister is still on the counter in the kitchen. When I told Ben how this had been bothering me, he even suggested that maybe she put something in the cookies. We all slept through whatever happened with Jacob. I don't know. It was just wrong somehow." She sounded flustered. "Am I being too much? I feel like it's my fault he's missing. Maybe I'm reaching. Looking for someone else to take the blame."

"I'll look into it. Just put that canister up where no one can touch it. I'll need to pick it up."

"Oh, Lord, what're you going to do? If you go to Wilma, she'll think I'm a nutcase."

"Don't worry about it. She'll never know you called. Now, put the canister up and stay calm. I'll get back to you."

Deke ended the call while Tara ripped off her pajama top and dragged on the sweatshirt. "We're going to pay Wilma Hambrick a visit." She shimmied out of the pajama bottom and into her jeans.

"Why would she do something like this?" He handed Tara her phone.

She led the way out of the room and down the stairs. "Maybe she didn't, but we're going to find out. The thing that gives me pause is that the woman is obsessed with getting a full-fledged police department for the Hollow. She wants desperately to be mayor. Who knows how far she'd go?"

Her cell sounded off again. *Collin.* "Hey," she said, on her way to the backdoor. "I was just about to call you."

"Well, we had another burglary," he said. "Deputy Wilhelm spotted the perpetrators fleeing the scene on his way back home."

Wilhelm was one of the deputies who had been sent to the Hollow to help. "Did they get away?" She walked out, waited for Deke to follow and locked the door.

"They did not. He got them and guess what? It is the Hand boys. Wilhelm is holding them at the office right now. They're handcuffed and stowed in the conference room. He said he'd hang around until one of us could get there."

"Tell Wilhelm to stay. We're going to need him," she warned Collin. "Meet me at the station."

"Already headed that way."

"Thanks. See you in three." She ended the call and passed along the news to Deke.

"Louise Hand is going to be pissed," he said, climbing into the passenger side of the Wagoneer.

"Louise will have to wait," Tara warned as she slid behind the wheel. "Hambrick comes first. At this point, we can't be sure just how far she intends to go." There was an off chance this theory was just that, a theory. But Tara didn't think so. The woman's pushiness and insistence had all come crashing in on Tara with Wright's call.

"She is one to obsess." Deke fastened his seat belt.

"I remember that Christmas parade year before last. She was in charge and wanted the elementary kids to have a big part. She drove me up the wall."

Tara started the engine. "Whatever she's done, I just hope everyone is okay."

"Wasn't there some rumor about how her husband died?"

"Yeah." Tara backed from the carport. "That's what scares the hell out of me."

Chapter Eighteen

By the time Tara and Deke arrived at the station, the twins were ready to spill their guts.

Tara and Collin sat in the conference room with the two black-haired, brown-eyed eighteen-year-olds who had been caught red-handed with a stolen laptop and cell phone from yet another Hollow residence. Their mother, Louise, sat next to her boys, quietly fuming.

"She hired us to shake things up," Edgar said. He glanced at his brother. "Wouldn't you say that's what she wanted?"

Elton nodded. "She said petty crimes. Just enough small-time trouble to make people start complaining about the lack of police support in the Hollow."

The longer Tara listened the angrier she grew. "You're stating," Tara reiterated, "that Wilma Hambrick hired you to cause trouble. To steal from people's homes."

"First," Louise spoke up sharply, "before my boys

say another word, you said their cooperation would make this go a lot easier for them. Let's not forget that."

Tara nodded. "You have my word." She looked to the boys then and motioned for them to go on.

Edgar nodded. "She said we'd end up in juvie since we just turned eighteen and had no criminal record. No big deal. She paid us five hundred bucks each for every hit."

Tara almost laughed. "What else did you do for her—besides the break-ins?"

The two stared at each other before Edgar said, "We'd like a lawyer now."

"Mom," Elton whined.

Louise's eyes rounded. "Oh God, what have you not told me?"

Tara held up her hands. "Call your lawyer. We can continue this later."

Tara walked out. Collin did the same.

"What now?" he asked once they were clear of the conference room door.

"Let them sweat," she said. The two would get no sympathy from her. "We have three missing people to find and I think it's safe to say we know where to start looking."

Hydrangea Place, 11:30 p.m.

WILMA HAMBRICK LIVED in a perfect little cottage on a tiny cul-de-sac with only one other house just off Main Street. Previously, she and her deceased husband, Gordon, had lived on a small farm just outside the Hollow. Wilma made no secret that she loved the little cottage on Hydrangea Place. When her husband had his stroke and became disabled, she begged him to allow her to sell the farm and move to the little cottage that had come up for sale. Gordon had refused. Although his body no longer served him as it once had, his mind remained unexpectedly sharp.

Not long after the cottage went up for sale, Gordon died of a heart attack. No one was surprised. In time, there had been rumors that Wilma stopped giving him his heart medication. Since the man was dead and buried, no one ever pursued the idea. Some even suggested they didn't blame poor Wilma. Gordon had been as mean as hell. Even his grown children had stayed away for the most part.

"You think she really killed her husband?" Deke asked.

Sitting in the dark with Deke was making Tara antsy after what went down in her kitchen. With the call from Wright and the news about the twins, everything else had gone on the back burner—until now, alone in the dark.

Focus. This was the first solid lead they'd gotten and Tara was praying it would pay off. Before she and Collin had gotten out of the substation, Louise Hand had called them back. The three had decided not to wait for the lawyer after all. Based on the statements made by the twins, Hambrick was guilty, for sure. She had ordered the boys to nab the Callaways, but they had refused. Considering her offer to pay them a lot more money, they figured she had found someone else for the job.

There was always the chance she had decided against the plot and had nothing to do with their disappearances. In the end, the break-ins and the missing Callaways might not be connected.

Tara hoped like hell they were and that Hambrick had the three stashed safely somewhere.

Tara and Deke had come in his truck. She had been concerned that Wilma would look out the window and spot her trademark Wagoneer. Collin was parked at the corner of Main and Hydrangea. He would head this way on Tara's signal.

"Maybe," Tara said in answer to Deke's question about Hambrick's husband. "Dad said if she did, he got what he deserved."

"If your dad said that," Deke noted, "her husband must have been a really bad man."

"I don't remember him, but I'm with you. If my dad said it, it's probably so."

Tara considered something else her dad had told her. "Dad said she sold the farm and bought this cottage. Then she took his insurance money and turned it into the showplace she wanted. She bought herself an expensive car and a whole new wardrobe. She travels all the time. Evidently there's plenty more since she paid the twins to promote her desire to be mayor."

"The longer I think about this," Deke said, "the more convinced I am that she might not be playing with a full deck. If that's the case and Jacob and his parents are in there being held hostage, I just hope they're okay."

"Maybe she only kills bad husbands." Tara wasn't sure she believed the woman had deprived her husband of his medicine, but if the Callaways were actually being held somewhere and she was the reason, she would feel differently.

The bedroom light—the last one on in the house—went out. Time to move. Tara wanted to catch the woman off guard.

"I'm going to the back door," she said. She turned to face him, though seeing his eyes in the dark was not happening. "Do not get out of this vehicle unless I say so. Having a civilian in an op could create serious consequences for me. Got it?"

He exhaled a big breath. "Got it."

"I mean it, Deke, do not get out of this truck."

"Okay, okay. I won't get out until you say so." He hesitated. "Unless I hear gunfire or see flames. Something extreme like that."

That was likely as good as his answer was going to get. Tara got out and moved quickly through the darkness. She'd dressed in her black sweats and pulled on a black beanie and tucked her blond hair into it. Her sneakers were black, so she was mostly concealed. They had parked a good distance from her house. The other house was dark too. Collin said the Bedwells were on a fourteen-day cruise and had asked him to drive by now and then. With them gone, Tara didn't have to worry about their big dog. He would likely be with a friend or at a kennel.

Tara made it to the yard. Wilma's gardens, as she called them, front and back, were like botanical parks. Massive blooming shrubs. All manner of blooming vines. The numerous layers of plants and shrubs created a perfect shield. Tara slipped around back and had a look around as best she could with only the moonlight for guidance. Based on the inactive real estate listing still online, the house had two bedrooms and a basement. Like a lot of older homes, the basement had an exterior entrance. Tara hoped Wilma hadn't closed it off.

If she'd added something in the cookies to put the Wrights to sleep, she could be drugging the Callaways to keep them pliable.

Tara couldn't help feeling as if she were on a movie set. The very idea of what the woman may have done…of what was happening at this very moment… was surreal. Tara had almost called her dad on the drive over. How could Wilma Hambrick have done this right under Tara's nose? While the whole community went on with life?

Things like this didn't happen in Dread Hollow.

Even the Treat Foster story wasn't as bizarre as this one.

In light of the possible alternatives, Tara really hoped the Callaways were safely tucked in this basement. That scenario was far better than the others.

At the bottom of the steps that led down to the basement entrance, Tara surveyed the door. She tested the knob. It was locked of course. There was no window in the door, so seeing inside was a no go.

She tried the knob again.

Damn it.

When she would have turned around, she felt the subtle change in the air around her.

Someone was behind her. Up one or two steps.

When she would have whipped around ready to fight, the creeper whispered, "Tara, it's me."

Deke.

She turned around, resisted the urge to punch him. "What the hell?" she whispered back.

He moved closer. Her body reacted. She wanted to punch herself for her inability to control the reaction.

"I can open it."

She grabbed him by the ears and pulled his head down to hers and muttered, "Why did you get out of the truck?"

"I thought about what you said about the basement entrance. I figured if it was locked, you'd be in a pickle."

A pickle? Really.

She wanted to stay mad but couldn't. "Well, you were right. I'm in a pickle."

"Lucky for you, I know how to get out of pickles when locked doors are involved."

She frowned. He grinned. She felt the movement against her hands. She dropped her hands and stepped aside. "Have at it."

She had no idea how meek and mild Deke Shepherd would know one single thing about picking locks, but she was more than happy for the assist.

He reached into his pocket and removed some-

thing, then both hands hovered around the doorknob.
Ten seconds later, he opened the door a crack.

She put a hand up when he would have gone in.
He leaned closer to her face and she whispered. "Stay
behind me."

Usually a warrant would be necessary to enter
someone's property, but there was a little excep-
tion called exigent circumstances whenever there
was imminent danger to life or property. Like now.
Hopefully.

Tara slipped into the basement. Deke stayed so
close she could feel his breath on her neck. The inky
darkness seemed to close in around them. The par-
tially open door allowed a sliver of moonlight to slice
across the floor. Concrete.

She stood still and listened for a full minute. No
sounds upstairs. She slipped her cell from the pocket
of her sweatpants. Holding her breath, she switched
on the flashlight app.

The room was small. The steps going up were
only a few feet to the right. Shelves covered the
available walls. All were lined with boxes and other
stuff. She moved left along the opposite wall until
she found another door. She gestured for Deke to do
his magic with the lock.

Deke considered the lock. He shrugged, then
whispered, "It's a deadbolt. A new one added to
allow the door to be locked from this side. I can try,
but…" He shrugged again.

Damn you, Wilma Hambrick.

Deke went to work on the lock. Tara kept an eye

on the door at the top of the steps on the other side of the room. The more she thought about Wilma pulling this off, the angrier she grew.

The seconds ticked off like hours. She glanced at Deke again and he finally shook his head.

Damn. The key had to be upstairs.

At this point, a good lawyer might say she had exceeded the limitations of exigent circumstances and maybe she had. For all they knew, Hambrick could be keeping her best recipes locked away in this room. It couldn't be very large.

What Tara needed was proof.

She got down on her hands and knees, put her face close to the concrete. There was a space beneath the door of about an inch. She edged close to that space and shined her light inside. She couldn't see a thing.

Taking a breath, she whispered, "Jacob! You in there?"

Deke didn't say anything or move. He probably thought she'd lost her mind.

"Jacob!" she whispered a little louder.

Time to try something else. She propped her phone up against the door so that the camera was aimed into the space below the door and toward whatever was beyond it. She tapped the screen, and the flash flickered and held in the darkness. When the flash died, she pulled up the newly captured image.

Her breath caught in her throat.

Inside the room, seated on the floor and leaning against one another were Jacob and his parents. Tape secured their mouths and they were bound together.

The dog, Jelly Bug, was curled up next to Jacob. All eyes were closed. No movement.

Heart racing, Tara scrambled to her feet and showed the image to Deke.

"Are they alive?" he whispered.

"They must be, or there wouldn't be a reason to secure their mouths."

"Son of a bitch!"

Tara put her hand over his mouth and called Collin. Whispering, she ordered him to come to the front door and go with the plan they'd come up with as a backup. He would warn Wilma of a fire at the neighbor's house. There was no fire obviously, but Wilma, startled in the middle of the night like this, would be out of sorts long enough for Collin to get her out of the house.

"Are you saying they're in her basement?" Collin echoed.

"I just said that." Tara gave herself a mental shake. What was up with the guy?

"Ha! Patricia was right. She said they were being held in a dark place."

Tara wanted to say something snarky, but damn, he was right. "Get ready to move," she murmured, keeping her voice as quiet as possible.

Tara shoved the phone into her pocket and retrieved her backup piece, a thirty-eight, from her ankle holster. She pulled Deke's face down to hers. "Stay right here at this door. Do you hear me? Do not move under any circumstances."

He nodded.

Tara started to pull away, but he stopped her, kissed her hard on the lips. "Tell me you love me," he murmured.

"I love you." Tears welled in her eyes. Why had she pretended not to all this time?

She pulled away from his touch and moved quickly and quietly up the stairs, praying none of the wooden steps would squeak. She made it to the top without a sound. At the door, she carefully tested the knob.

Unlocked.

She left the door cracked and waited.

The pounding came a minute later.

"Ms. Hambrick! It's Deputy Porch. There's a fire next door." He pounded again. Long and hard. "Ms. Hambrick, wake up! There's a fire next door!"

Tara heard the woman stumbling about. Lights came on. Tara eased back into the darkness.

"What?" Hambrick called out.

"It's Deputy Porch. There's a fire next door. You need to get out of the house. The fire department is en route."

Muttering under her breath, Hambrick flipped the locks on her door. She opened it. "What's on fire?"

"Wilma Hambrick," he said, "you are under arrest for the abduction of the Callaway family."

Tara moved then. Slipping silently through the kitchen and into the dining room that adjoined the living room. Hambrick's back was to her.

"Collin Porch, are you inebriated?" Hambrick demanded. "How dare you come to my house in the middle of the night making such accusations!"

"Put your hands up, Ms. Hambrick." Tara was behind her before she could turn around. Unlike Collin, she had her weapon in hand.

Hambrick turned around, stumbled back, bumping into Collin.

"Where's the key to the room in the basement?"

Her hands in the air, Hambrick said, "Under my pillow."

"Cuff her and call for an ambulance," Tara told Collin.

She rushed to the bedroom and found the key under the pillow. Running now, Tara hurried down the steps and to the door where Deke waited.

She passed the key to him and he opened the door.

Tara went to the Callaways and checked the carotid pulse for each member of the family. "They're alive."

Thank God. Thank God.

By the time Deke and Tara had the three freed, they were trying to rouse, but whatever drug Hambrick had given them kept them groggy. Tara was grateful when the ambulance arrived and took them to the hospital in East Ridge. Thankfully, they took the dog too.

Hambrick had provided the drug she used to sedate them at night.

Tara and Deke followed the ambulance. Collin would transport Hambrick to holding at County. Deputy Wilhelm was already en route with the twins.

East Ridge Hospital
Sunday, May 7, 2:30 a.m.

THE CALLAWAY FAMILY had been thoroughly examined and were deemed to be unharmed beyond the ligature marks from their bindings. Because of the drug, the doctor felt it best to keep the family the rest of the night for observation. He'd also given the go-ahead for the father to be interviewed. Deke was spending time with Jacob and his mom. Another deputy had taken Jelly Bug to a local vet clinic.

Tara had called Agent Hanson so he could be involved in the interview. She had decided he wasn't such a bad guy after all. Everyone had a history and everyone had a motive for their actions. Herself included.

Tara pulled a chair up next to Callaway's bedside. She was too tired at this point to continue standing. Her blisters were stinging. Hanson stood at the foot of the bed.

Callaway's rights had been explained to him and he had waived his right to an attorney.

"Mr. Callaway," Tara began, "you'll need to write up an official statement once you're out of the hospital, but for now, we'd like to ask a few questions to clarify certain aspects of the case."

"Whatever you need." The man stared at his hands. "I'm embarrassed at what I've allowed my family to be a part of."

"We understand how you came to be at the property on Falling Rock Trace. Witnesses have stated that you were hired to do lawn service."

He nodded. "That's right. I cut the grass and any overgrown shrubs once a month from May until October last year."

"How did you find the cave?" Tara asked next.

"My wife was very sick last summer and fall. She had breast cancer. This one day, I was supposed to go to the house to work, and I took the dog with me. Jelly Bug was just a pup then and I hated to leave her. You know how puppies are. My wife was far too ill to deal with that. I thought it was a big yard, no problem, right? I figured it would be fine. And all went well until I was finished and loading up the mower. I think the dog maybe saw a rabbit or something and took off into the woods."

"You went after the dog," Tara suggested.

He nodded. "When I found her, she was barking into the cave. She was afraid to go inside, but I guess the rabbit or whatever didn't mind."

"What made you go into the cave?"

He shrugged. "Plain old curiosity. I used to love caving with my father when I was a kid. I went back to my truck, put Jelly Bug in the cab and got my flashlight. Once I went into the cave, the farther I dared go, the more interesting the place was. I'd never found a cave like that one."

"Did you find anything in the cave?" This from Hanson.

Callaway nodded. "Yes, sir. I came upon what looked like a campsite. Someone had lived there a long time ago, but he was long dead." He made a face. "I didn't touch him. But I did look through his stuff. That's when I found the money."

"How much of the money did you take?" Tara asked.

"The first time, I took forty thousand. Exactly the amount we needed to pay my wife's medical bills. It was wrong, I know, but it felt like a godsend."

"But then you went back recently," Hanson pointed out.

Callaway nodded. "The cancer is back. We haven't told Jacob yet, but she starts treatments again next week. The doctor warned us the treatment would be more this time, so I took fifty. I'm not sorry I did," he admitted. "I'm just sorry I couldn't take care of my family on my own."

"How did you end up in Wilma Hambrick's basement?" Hambrick was refusing to talk. She'd lawyered up. The twins stood by their assertion they'd turned down the job.

"She knew about our medical bills and came to see me after I got off work at the hatchery one day a couple weeks ago. She asked me if I would like to earn ten thousand dollars. I said yeah, sure. She said she needed my family to pretend to be abducted. She wants a real police department and she thought if she showed you how difficult it was to take care of a real crime, you'd help her make that happen."

"What did you say to her proposition?"

"At first I said yes." He shrugged. "I thought the

extra money would be a good cushion if the fifty wasn't enough."

"Why didn't you just go back to the cave for more money?" Tara asked.

"Because she said if I didn't do what she asked, she would start rumors about me and my wife. We'd lose our jobs and maybe our son. I know how much influence she has around here. I was afraid to say no."

Tara thought about that for a moment. "Jacob said you and your wife were surprised when those men showed up to take you. Why is that?"

"Krissy didn't want to do it. She didn't care what Wilma threatened to do. She said Delilah would never believe anything Wilma said. So I called Ms. Hambrick up and told her we weren't doing it. She said it was too late. The men she'd hired to play the kidnappers were coming. I tried to get home in time to take Krissy and Jacob and run, but I was too late."

Damn. Obviously Wilma Hambrick had gone over the edge.

"Why did she take Jacob from the Wright home?"

"She said she heard how upset he was and she couldn't bear the idea of him being without us any longer. She made us tell her the kinds of cookies Jacob wouldn't eat. It was surreal. She's lost it. She drugged the Wrights and told Jacob she could bring him to us."

"I'm sorry this happened to you and your family," Tara said. "And I'm even more sorry your wife's cancer is back."

He nodded, his face telling the story of the sadness he felt.

"I just have one more question, Mr. Callaway," Hanson said.

Callaway met the other man's gaze. "Yes?"

"Why didn't you take it all? The money in the cave, I mean."

Callaway looked away. "I'm just a regular guy. I work hard. I love my family. But I'm no thief. And I'm damned sure not greedy."

Tara stood. "Thank you, Mr. Callaway. We'll need your help as well as your family's to ensure Ms. Hambrick doesn't get away with what she's done."

"We'll cooperate fully." He glanced at the agent then back to Tara. "What about the money? I can pay it back. It'll take me the rest of my life, but I'm willing to do it. And just so you know, my family had nothing to do with what I did. I acted alone."

The fact that the man wanted to protect his family was further proof of how much he loved them.

"Considering the money is tied to a robbery more than thirty years old," Hanson said, "the statute of limitations has expired on the federal level as well as the state level. Found money has its own rules. You turn it over to the police and wait. If no one claims it, it's returned to you."

Tara smiled, her respect for the agent growing.

"What're you saying?" Callaway asked, his expression hopeful.

"I'm saying you didn't break any laws. The fifty

thousand has been placed in police custody. If no one claims it, it will be returned to you."

"Won't the bank claim it?"

Hanson shook his head. "That bank closed years ago. The account holders were covered by the bank's insurance."

"But I didn't turn over the other money. The first time."

Hanson glanced at Tara and shrugged. "Do you know anything about other money? Besides what we found in the cave? We have no idea how much Foster spent of the money he stole."

Tara shrugged as well. "You're right. There's no way to know." She turned to Callaway. "What money?"

Callaway's mouth trembled and his voice broke as he managed a thank-you.

Hanson gave him a nod and left the room.

"Take care of yourself and your family, Mr. Callaway. Jacob is a great kid."

Tara left the room. Hanson waited in the corridor for her.

He thrust out his hand. "It was a pleasure working with you, Deputy Norwood."

Tara shook his hand. "I like you better than I wanted to," she admitted.

He laughed. "I get that a lot."

"You did a good thing in there."

"The guy did me a favor. I just solved a thirty-year-old cold case. I may get a promotion." He gave Tara a salute and walked away.

Tara found Deke stepping out of Jacob and his mom's room. He turned and smiled at her. "Hey. Everything go okay?"

"Callaway won't face any charges," she told him, knowing he needed to hear that news.

"That's great."

"Hambrick won't get off so easy." Tara intended to see to that.

"She shouldn't," Deke agreed.

They walked quietly through the hospital and on to the parking area where she'd left her Wagoneer.

"What now?" he asked.

"Now," Tara said, "I'm taking you home and then I'm going home. We both have a lot to think about."

"True. Don't forget lunch with your dad tomorrow."

"Today, technically."

"Today," Deke agreed.

Tara climbed behind the wheel; Deke slid into the passenger seat. She pointed her Wagoneer in the direction of home.

The past six days had clarified a lot of things.

Tomorrow she intended to see if those changes were going to be part of their futures. But first, they both needed sleep and time apart to think.

Except it was already tomorrow and her mind was made up.

"I changed my mind," she announced.

Deke turned to her. "About what?"

"I'm taking you home with me, Deke Shepherd, and this time I'm never letting you go."

He smiled. Reached for her hand. "Good, because I'm planning on marrying you, Tara Norwood. The sooner, the better."

At the next light, they kissed. "Good," she said, repeating his word, "because I want my dad to walk me down the aisle."

* * * * *

#2157 MAVERICK DETECTIVE DAD
Silver Creek Lawmen: Second Generation • by Delores Fossen
When Detective Noah Ryland and Everly Monroe's tragic pasts make them targets of a vigilante killer, they team up to protect her young daughter and stop the murders. But soon their investigation unleashes a series of vicious attacks...along with reigniting the old heat between them.

#2158 MURDER AT SUNSET ROCK
Lookout Mountain Mysteries • by Debra Webb
A ransacked house suggests that Olivia Ballard's grandfather's death was no mere accident. Deputy Detective Huck Monroe vows to help her uncover the truth. But as dark secrets surrounding Olivia's family are exposed, she'll have to trust the man who broke her heart to stay alive.

#2159 SHROUDED IN THE SMOKIES
A Tennessee Cold Case Story • by Lena Diaz
Former detective Adam Trent is stunned to learn his cold case victim is alive. But Skylar Montgomery is still very much in danger—and desperate for Adam's help. Their investigation leads them to one of Chattanooga's most powerful families...and a vicious web of mystery, intrigue and murder.

#2160 TEXAS BODYGUARD: WESTON
San Antonio Security • by Janie Crouch
Security Specialist Weston Patterson risks everything to keep his charges safe. But protecting wealthy Kayleigh Delacruz is his biggest challenge yet. She doesn't want a bodyguard. But as the kidnapping threat grows, she'll do anything—even trust Weston's expertise—to survive.

#2161 DIGGING DEEPER
by Amanda Stevens
When Thora Graham awakens inside a coffin-like box with no memory of how she got there, Deputy Police Chief Will Dresden, the man she left fifteen years ago, follows the clues to save her life. Their twisted reunion becomes a race against time to stop a serial killer's vengeful scheme.

#2162 K-9 HUNTER
by Cassie Miles
Piper Comstock and her dog, Izzy, live a solitary, peaceful life. Until her best friend is targeted by an assassin. US Marshal Gavin McQueen knows the truth— a witness in protection is compromised. It's dangerous to recruit a civilian to help with the investigation. But is the danger to Piper's life...or Gavin's heart?

HARLEQUIN
PLUS

Try the best multimedia
subscription service for romance
readers like you!

Read, Watch and Play.

Experience the easiest way to get
the romance content you crave.

Start your **FREE TRIAL** at
<u>www.harlequinplus.com/freetrial</u>.